MW01124855

# Framed for Murder

*A Cozy Cottage Mystery*

## Lori Hawthorne Ponton

**Copyright © 2017 by Lori Hawthorne Ponton**
**All Right reserved in the  United States 2017**

Published by The Creative Short Book Writers Project
Printing Platform: Createspace
Distribution USA: Amazon.com

Cover Design by SelfPubBookCovers.com/RLSather
Author photo copyright © 2015 by Lori Hawthorne Ponton

**ISBN-13: 978-1979740593**
**ISBN-10: 1979740593**

# ~ INTRODUCTION ~

Emmy Weston is a historical designer in a small Virginia town. Her days are normally filled with researching the history of a client's home, furniture or antique collections. Discovering hidden rewards and connections between the items and the family has its challenges....especially when a mystery surfaces in a secret compartment or behind a wall.

When Emmy and her husband Sam decide to buy her grandmother's home in the country, the nostalgic idea of repairing an old family cottage with hidden potential may turn out to be more challenging than rewarding. Clues soon lead them to a local town leader and Emmy's missing family heirloom.

# ~CONTENTS~

# Framed for Murder

*A Cozy Cottage Mystery*

Lori Hawthorne Ponton

~~~ Chapter 1 ~~~

Emma "Emmy" Weston stood outside the small
gate and admired the cottage from a safe distance.
Several roof shingles hung loose, others lay
scattered around the ground. The narrow casement
windows displayed several broken panes. The
paint, peeling and faded, barely covered the
shingles that wrapped the cottage. The porch, once
a comfortable shady spot to rest, sagged in places.
The front yard was no longer pristine. It was now

choked with weeds and long-ago forgotten garden tools lay rusting in the grass. Slate stepping stones were cracked or missing. The front door stood ajar.

"What a mess." said the male voice from behind her. "Not the kind of place I really like." Samuel Weston, Emmy's husband, preferred newly constructed homes.

*Place?* It's not just a *place*, Emmy thought in dismay. It was her Grandmother's home; one Emmy enjoyed visiting frequently during her childhood summers. The swing was still there, hanging from a tree. Emmy closed her eyes and took a deep breath. The intense fragrance of honeysuckle filled her with happiness. All she needed were sandals, a glass of iced tea, homemade brownies, and she was 12 again.

"Sam, you promised. If we don't make an offer soon, it will be gone. Bought by someone else, torn down, or left to collapse; it will be gone."

Sam sighed. "Let's go inside." He knew what the house meant to Emmy, and the memories it held for her. She was, after all, the only granddaughter and her Grandmother's namesake.

Emma Cooper, known as "Granny" to all, and her husband Charles built the cottage in the late

1930's in Central Virginia. The arched wooden
front door and decorative half-timbers set their
home apart from the neighbors. Charles, a farmer
and coal miner, handcrafted many of the cottage's
details. On the exterior, he built the wooden
shutters and front door. On the interior, he built the
bookcases and kitchen cabinets. Even Sam could
appreciate the workmanship Grandpa Charles left
for future generations.

"Watch your step, honey." Sam took Emmy's
hand to steady her. They navigated over the
uneven slate, pushing their way through the
overgrown front yard. Mounting the shaky stairs,
they stepped into the front hallway. Their eyes
soon adjusted to the dim interior.

"Wow," they both said at the same time; Sam,
because of the damp, musty smell, and Emmy,
because of the emptiness. The job ahead came into
focus as they scanned the front rooms: peeling
paint, rotted floor boards, crumbling plaster and
water stains.

"Bless you," Emmy said in response to Sam's
sneeze. "I guess it's a little dusty in here."

*A little?* Sam thought, looking around. *It's a lot dusty and it's going to be a lot of work and a lot of money to fix up. We can just build –*

"Oh!" Emmy's voice came from the kitchen. Sam ran in her direction, avoiding rotted floor boards as best he could.

"Are you OK?" Sam rounded the corner and laughed. There, by the pantry, stood his bride of five years, pulling cobwebs off her face. He laughed again and admired her pretty face.

"Yes, just help me, please. You know I don't like spiders." He brushed the silky web away from her face and hair.

"Then we should just build a new house without spiders." He grinned. Her look said otherwise.

Emmy knew buying and restoring her grandparent's home would be quite a chore; one she was willing to tackle if Sam was. Her design background and his handyman skills would be put to the test, but with a personal stake in the project she knew they could handle it.

Back in the front area, Emmy's eyes scanned the sparsely furnished rooms. A few dusty books lay on the shelves that used to hold a collection of stories. Keys were missing from the upright piano whose tunes used to hang in the air. A mirror that used to reflect the twinkle in Granny's eyes was propped in the corner. Not only did the rooms appear empty, they *felt* empty.

Sam paused in the doorway between the living room and dining room and sneezed again.

"Are you ready to go? We need to talk about making that offer." Sam tried to wipe the dust from his hands, but the more he tried the more dust he stirred.

Dust covered everything in its path – furnishings, rugs, light fixtures, door knobs. Even the bare walls were dusty. Walls that used to bustle with family photos now stared back blankly. Emmy still wanted to roam around a little more, even in the stale dusty air.

"Almost; give me another minute."

Emmy headed carefully upstairs. The steps groaned but otherwise held her weight. Her hands made fresh prints in the railing dust as she held on. She stepped carefully in the foot prints Sam must have made earlier as he roamed through the house. She let her mind wander. *What a beauty the staircase will be when refinished.*

"Honey, I'm going outside on the front porch." Sam needed to breathe more than dampness and dust.

"OK. I won't be long. I just want to see my room."

Her room was where she stayed during her summer visits. Like the other rooms downstairs, it was sparse on furnishings, but full of memories. Instead of painted plaster walls, her room had daisy-patterned wall paper. Daisies were nature's way of sending smiles, Granny used to say. Even now, faded, the daisies made Emmy smile. Still smiling, she walked over to the window and peered down at Sam. She admired that he was coming around to "liking" the house. *Soon you will love it,* she said to herself.

"Be down in a second," she yelled through the window. There was no need to open the sash since several glass panes were missing.

Emmy headed to the closet; one of her favorite spots in the room. It was a large closet and she often "camped" in there with a pillow, iced tea, brownies and a book. She always had a book. It was an escape into worlds unknown. She could be anything and go anywhere she wanted. A princess on a deserted island? *Yes*. A farm girl in a castle? *Yes*. A few books remained in the closet, haphazardly tossed on the floor. She noticed one of her favorites and bent to pick it up, tucking the note that fell out into her pocket. Smiling, she turned when she heard footsteps coming into the room.

"Oh, Sam, *Heidi* was one of my fav – who are you?"

The hit to the head knocked Emmy out and she fell hard to the floor. The wooden banister post delivered a cloud of dust and a thunderous noise as it hit the floor.

"Emmy? Is everything alright?" Sam yelled up to the broken window panes. "Emmy?"

Sam took the steps two at a time, slipping on the dusty covering. Ignoring the large footprints in the hallway leading to the back window, he found Emmy stirring on her bedroom floor. As he reached for her, gently smoothing her hair, she whispered.

"He took Granny's pocket watch."

# ～ Chapter 2 ～

The aroma of fresh-baked cookies swirled through the air. Jenn held the plate close to her as she approached the cottage. The afternoon was sunny and bright with a cool breeze rustling the new growth on the plants. Even the choking weeds swayed with the breeze. It was perfect spring weather for the central Virginia town of Middlebridge.

The small gate stood open beckoning her to come in. Jenn stood there taking in the sad sight of the cottage. "Hello?" She paused, not wanting to be surprised by something scurrying or slithering from the weeds across her path. "Emmy…Sam?"

Jennifer Haynes was one of Emmy's best childhood friends. They met in fourth grade when Jenn moved with her family from Pennsylvania to Virginia. Through their love of Barbies and books, Emmy and Jenn became fast friends. Jenn spent many days at the cottage when Emmy visited her grandparents. Giggles were paramount as they "camped" in the closet planning their day's adventure. The memories of sharing dreams, laughing and eating brownies in the closet made her smile.

*Maybe they're walking in the back yard.* Jenn thought, since no one answered her greeting. She made her way through the weeds and around the side of the cottage. She stopped briefly once she spotted the swing in the old oak tree. It moved gently, swaying with the breeze. She and Emmy had spent many lazy afternoons swinging back and forth, sometimes sharing the seat. Granny could see them from a small window; always keeping an eye on them. Jenn smiled at the thought of Granny's face peering out from the window. *It will be nice to have life back in the cottage.*

The side yard gave way to a large back yard, surrounded by peaks of the Blue Ridge Mountains rising in the distance. Many summer sunsets faded behind those peaks during young Jenn's and Emmy's time at the cottage. Just like the front yard, stepping stones were cracked or missing and Jenn stepped cautiously.

"Hello?" Jenn said again, louder. This time she headed toward the back of the property where a small shed stood, its door hanging off the hinges. Granny and Grandpa Charles stored a variety of items here: gardening tools, canning supplies, baskets and flower pots. Jenn and Emmy had helped Granny plant peonies in the pots and carried vegetables from the garden in the baskets.

The garden was a source of pride to Granny and Grandpa Charles. A labor of love, it was big enough to feed their family of four with plenty left over for the neighbors. Granny was all too happy to share or trade vegetables for homemade jams and pies. They kept the garden as long as they could; eventually it became too big for just the two of them. As they aged and their health deteriorated, so did the garden.

Just like the cottage, the years had not been kind to the shed. Most of the baskets and flower pots had seen better days. Jenn moved a few flower pots out of the way with her foot as she walked closer to the shed. A sudden movement in the weeds stopped Jenn in her tracks. Her breathing slowed; nothing moved except her eyes as they scanned the area.

"Oh, silly boy," she sighed, hearing a meow as one of the village cats pranced by. She reached down and gave the grey and white tabby a loving touch. "You startled me." Jenn remembered the cookies she was carrying, and decided the shed could wait. Turning toward the cottage, she never saw the shadowy figure retreat further back into the darkness of the shed. She made her way carefully back through the weeds, around an old birdbath and over a small rock pile to the back porch. The rotted floor boards offered a precarious trip to the back door which stood slightly open.

"Hello?" Jenn peered inside then stepped into the mudroom. The sunlight beamed through broken window panes and danced off old canning jars and their lids. *Mmmm...green beans, tomato sauce and peas,* Jenn fondly remembered. *How I'd love to have some of Granny's good food.*

Laying the plate of cookies on the counter as she walked into the kitchen, Jenn looked around. She and Emmy loved spending time with Granny, playing with their Barbies, watching her bake delicious things. Sometimes, when they were old enough, they helped Granny bake her famous brownies. Those brownies were a favorite of many folks in town. Jenn smiled as she remembered Granny's response to repeated requests for the recipe. *"Oh, it's just the usual recipe. Then, I add a lot of laughter, a splash of singing and a little bit of love."*

Sighing, Jenn continued around the kitchen running her fingers along the cabinets. Admiring the craftsmanship of Grandpa Charles' handiwork, she opened each cabinet. He was always building or fixing something for the cottage. The cabinets were in decent shape and could certainly be salvaged during a renovation. The thought of renovating the cottage made Jenn smile, and reminded her why she stopped by.

"Emmy…Sam? It's me, Jenn." She noticed footprints and headed to the front rooms, carefully maneuvering around rotted floor boards. Pulling cobwebs away from her face, she picked up some dusty books and set them on a bookcase in the living room. She was about to walk into the small dining area adjacent to the kitchen when she heard a cough, and then a low mummer. Familiar voices? Emmy's and Sam's voices? She stood there silently, eyes wide, listening.

"Don't move too quickly, Emmy. You'll no doubt have a good knot on the side of your head." Sam smoothed her hair, gently.

"I don't understand. Who was that? Why did he take Granny's pocket watch?" Struggling, Emmy sat up slowly. "Did you see him?"

"No, honey, I didn't. I heard a loud noise, a thud really, and ran upstairs. You were already on the floor. When I – sshhh, did you hear that?" Sam listened carefully, pulling Emmy close to him. Was this person coming back for something else?

Sam picked up the wooden bannister post and motioned for Emmy to sit still. Stepping into the hallway, he slid into a little alcove with a view down the stairs. *Come up here and you'll get a taste of your own medicine!* Sam's heart was racing. Slowly, he stepped out of the alcove and onto the landing. Making his way quietly down the first few steps, he sees Jenn step into view.

"Emmy…Sam?" As Sam relaxes, the wooden post falls from his hands. "Jenn…"

"Sam!" Both Jenn and Emmy are startled at the sound of the wooden post tumbling down the steps.

"It's OK! Emmy, Jenn. It's OK! Jenn, come help me with Emmy." Jenn raced up the stairs, trying not to slip on their dusty covering. She and Sam sat with Emmy, talking softly about the incident, while Emmy regained her thoughts.

"It's a mystery why anyone would want to hurt you, or take Granny's pocketwatch," Jenn frowned. "Do you have any ideas?" She reached for and held Emmy's hand. Caressing the top, Jenn looked at her and the daisy-patterned wall paper. A smile brightened her face.

"None." Emmy shook her head. "Oh, that hurts."

"You've had quite a hit." Sam stood up. "Let's get you out of here." As Sam and Jenn guided Emmy out of the bedroom, all three noticed the large footprints in the hallway leading to the back window. "I guess that's the escape route he took."

Looking closer, Jenn took a few mental notes before the sun went down casting shadows through the cottage. She wanted to be sure she remembered everything about the wooden post, the footsteps, and the pocket watch. They would call the police later that evening once Emmy was settled.

As they headed to the front door, Jenn remembered the cookies she left in the kitchen. "I'll get them," Sam offered. Emmy and Jenn made their way out the front door, across the front porch, and over the cracked stepping stones. Sam grabbed the plate of cookies, sampling one as he hustled back through the cottage.

From the darkness of the shed, eyes followed Sam as he caught up to the girls at the front gate.

~~~ Chapter 3 ~~~

Middlebridge, one of the oldest towns in
Central Virginia, was a charming place with most
of its town and farm land nestled in the arms of the
Blue Ridge Mountains. The fresh air seemed to
beckon to anyone who dared: breathe deeply. If
one's taste did not lean toward quaint or cozy
villages, the place proved a disappointment. There
were no big department stores, no shopping malls,
no movie theatres. Other than a small post office

and one bank, the places of business that existed were family-run cafes, thrift stores and antique shops. Middlebridge was a beautiful place to visit. If you were lucky, your family visited generations ago, established roots, and never left.

Growing up, Emmy loved visiting her grandparents in Middlebridge for the summer. She and her cousins, if they were along for the summer visit, read, and played "I Spy" until the curves of the mountain roads forced them to stop. No one wanted to be queasy when arriving at Granny's and Grandpa Charles' and risk missing a warm homemade brownie. Emmy's older cousins – by two and three years – Matthew and Robert – didn't care that she was a girl; she played the same games and climbed the same trees. She also kept them out of trouble. At some point during the summers, no one knew what happened to a missing ball (Matt lost it in the creek), a broken shed window (Robbie tried juggling rocks), or the trampled flower bed (both boys wrestling). An extra brownie from the boys was Emmy's reward.

Driving to Middlebridge instinctively slows down the quick daily pace. Flat roads bend into curves and short ornamental evergreens turn into towering loblolly pines, gently swaying a welcoming "hello." The slower pace is what drew Emmy and Sam back to visit Jenn and Steve, and look at the cottage. Now they had to find out who would try to hurt Emmy and steal a family heirloom.

"Well hello everyone!" said Steve Haynes, Jenn's husband. He turned from the gas grill to greet them. "I didn't expect to see you until – what happened?" Sam and Jenn led Emmy in the side door and to the overstuffed chair by the fireplace.

"Someone was in Granny's cottage and knocked Emmy out. She has a good knot on her head." Jenn filled a glass with ice water, handing it to Emmy. "Drink slowly."

"I'm okay. Really. Just a little shaken." Emmy sipped the water, grateful for its coolness as it settled her stomach.

"I still want the doctor to check you out," Sam insisted. "Then I'm going back to look for Granny's pocket watch."

"I'll call the doctor now." Jenn brought Emmy a cool wet cloth placing it on her forehead, then stepped into the kitchen with her cell phone.

"What about Granny's pocket watch?" asked Steve.

"The jerk who hurt Emmy stole Granny's pocket watch." Sam held Emmy's hand. "Why, we don't know, but I'm going back to check around the cottage to see if he dropped it somewhere." He got up, headed to the door and looked at Steve. "I could use your help."

Steve and Sam had become friends through the friendship of their wives. They were in each other's weddings, vacationed together, and renovated parts of Jenn's and Steve's home. If Sam and Emmy could purchase Granny's cottage, they planned to work on that together, too.

"Wait a minute, Buddy." Steve held up his hand. "You can't go back there. Someone was assaulted and property was stolen. It's a crime scene now." As much as Sam hated to admit it, he knew Steve was right. They couldn't go back tonight.

Steve Haynes was an investigator with the Middlebridge sheriff's office. He grew up not far from Middlebridge and knew the area well. He met Jenn a few years ago through his young nephew who was one of her 6th grade history students.

Staying in the area after they married allowed Jenn to continue teaching the students she cared so passionately about. Steve's investigative skills kept him busy and involved in many of the local friends and families he grew up with. The incident at Granny's cottage was one he wished he wasn't involved with. Crimes involving close friends and family were the hardest to handle.

Steve glanced at Sam and Emmy. "You know you'll have to stop any real estate transactions and renovation plans until things are cleared up."

"But how can we – ." Emmy started to protest, but realized it was no use. "Another delay, but I guess you're right."

Jenn brought Emmy another wet cloth and some warm broth; she was feeling better. When the doctor called, Emmy was able to answer questions coherently and Jenn confirmed with the doctor that a mild headache was the worst of any concerns. Rest and no physical exertion was what Emmy needed.

"We'll all rest tonight and start fresh in the morning." Jenn and Emmy headed upstairs.

~~~~~

Staring at the cottage, Steve took a pen from his pocket, opened a small notebook and began to write. "Tell me again – slower this time – exactly what happened."

Emmy nodded, still bewildered at what happened yesterday afternoon. "Sam and I want to purchase the cottage, fix it up and raise our family in it." Emmy moved along the front part of the fence, pausing at the gate. "We stopped here on our way to your place so we could look around." All four stepped through the open gate and made their way to the front porch.

"We walked through the downstairs and I went upstairs to my old room while Sam went to sit on the front porch. Once in my room, I picked up a few books from the floor and put some of them in the closet, heard what I thought was Sam, turned around and WHACK! Some guy hit me with a wooden banister." Steve led the group into the front hallway.

"When I heard a thud, I ran inside, up the steps and found Emmy in her room on the floor," Sam continued. "She told me that someone took Granny's pocket watch."

Standing in the front room, they let their eyes adjust to the dim surroundings.

"I'll take a quick look around while the rest of you stay right here." Steve unholstered his gun. He came back in a few minutes then headed upstairs. Sam, Emmy and Jenn looked around but remained silent. Steve spent a long time upstairs.

"I'll get someone out here to look at things," Steve said after rejoining the group. "Maybe we can find some fingerprints. I doubt we find evidence of forced entry since the cottage is wide open." They headed outside.

Steve looked back at Emmy. "You said you put books back in the closet – one being Heidi, I think."

"Yes, it's my favorite book and I hated seeing it on the floor."

Steve frowned. "It wasn't in the closet. In fact, no books were in the closet."

Emmy looked confused. "That's not right. A handful of books were in the closet on the floor; nowhere else."

Steve shook his head. "Books were strewn over the bedroom floor. Some had pages torn out. Did you put up a fight with the intruder?"

"No." Emmy continued. "I picked up a book, put it in the closet, turned around and was hit on the head."

"Well," Steve started. "It appears someone came back looking for something."

"Yeah…but what?" asked Jenn. "What could someone possibly be looking for?"

# ~~ Chapter 4 ~~

Like many small towns, Middlebridge had its share of busy bodies. Nothing serious, just a few harmless elderly ladies who were determined to know anything and everything about anyone and everyone. The incident with Emmy at her grandparents' cottage was no exception.

"Such a shame, what happened at the old Cooper cottage." Ms. Kate sipped her hot tea and shook her head.

"I know. Granny would be so disappointed."
Ms. Tess, setting her coffee down, took a bite of
her cinnamon crumb muffin, savoring its aroma.

"I heard some things were stolen but no one
knows what or who took them." Ms. Helen joined
her friends at the small café table with her coffee.
"And, Emmy fell down the stairs!"

Not to be outdone, Ms. Tess pursed her lips.
"Well, I heard she was hit on the head and a trail
of blood was found all through the cottage. What a
mess that will be to clean up."

"Oh no, dear," Mrs. Kate added shaking her
head. "She chased the thief outside, through the
weeds, tripped on the stepping stones and hit her
head on an old ceramic planter. Nearly died on the
spot!"

The three friends continued chatting, tsk-tsking
about current events, finishing their coffee and tea.
As they made plans to meet at The Middle Café
again next week, the Sheriff walked by.

"Mornin' ladies." Sheriff Morgan smiled and
tipped his hat. "Nice to see you all."

Sheriff William Morgan was well liked in
Middlebridge. He and his family moved to the area
over 20 years ago. After solving a local murder

quickly, he became a trusted part of the community and many treated him like he was part of their own family.

Ms. Tess, anxious to be the first to speak, waved her long boney hand in the air. "Oh Sheriff! Isn't it just awful about what happened to poor Emmy? Here only a short time and already making town news."

The Sheriff sighed softly to himself, placed his order and walked over to the three friends. Not wanting to get into a long conversation, his answer was short and polite.

"Yes, ma'am."

"Who could've done this? Who *would've* done this? Have you caught anyone? Do you know their name?" Ms. Helen barely breathed between each question.

"Well, no. But rest assured, we…" the Sheriff started.

"Give him a chance," interrupted Ms. Kate. "No one can outsmart the Sheriff." She smiled sweetly up at him.

"Thank you, ma'am." Seeing his chance to escape a more in-depth conversation, he added, "We'll do our best to solve this crime quickly. I'm on my way to the cottage now." He smiled, nodded goodbye, picked up his order, and hurried out of the café.

While they waited for the Sheriff to arrive, Jenn, Emmy, and Sam chatted quietly and Steve continued to write in his notebook. Steve took meticulous notes and paid attention to every crime detail. It was one of the qualities Sam shared with Steve. Sam's attention to detail during renovation projects meant the cottage would be in good hands. But first, he and Emmy had to help figure out what happened before the cottage could belong to them.

As Sam listened half-heartedly to Jenn and Emmy's conversation, he watched Steve intently. Words began to fill pages in Steve's small notebook as he paced back and forth. He looked up at the windows and around the weed-choked side of the cottage as his hand rested on his weapon. In his mind, Sam tried to follow Steve's actions. *He's scanning the area…*Sam glanced around. *…almost like he expects someone to be lurking about somewhere on the property.*

A patrol car pulled up to the cottage and Sheriff Morgan stepped out. His dancing blue-grey eyes and lively manner belied his years. His slightly protruding stomach was proof of many visits to The Middle Café; more visits than he cared to admit. He brushed crumbs off of his shirt as he stepped through the gate to greet everyone.

"I see you're hard at work Steve," the Sheriff said as he hugged Jenn hello.

He shook hands with Emmy and Sam. "It's good to see you both again. I'm sorry to hear the welcoming committee was a little less than cordial." A smile spread across his weathered face. "Let's see what we can do to fix that so new life can be breathed into the cottage. I know your grandparents would approve of that. Especially your Granny."

They carefully entered the cottage and Steve took them through recreating their steps. Emmy's mind ran over questions. *Who was looking for something? What were they looking for? Did Emmy throw a wrench in their plan, or did they mean to harm her?*

The group looked around, all noticing something different. A lamp with a broken shade, books on the shelves and on the floor, a mirror standing in the corner. And footprints. Footprints in the dust that covered the wood floors. Footprints that paraded from room to room, crisscrossing, and leading up the stairs.

"How many people have been through here?" A bewildered look crept across Sheriff Morgan's face.

"Just the three of us." Sam pointed to himself, Emmy, and Jenn. "And whoever knocked out Emmy."

"Well, these must be his prints." Steve motioned toward the largest footprints, obvious boot prints. No one else standing there was wearing boots.

The sheriff stayed with the group while Steve headed to the kitchen. Though the sun was out and shining, the dirty, neglected windows and the lack of electricity made the kitchen too dark to see much. The beam from Steve's flashlight cast long shadows across the wooden cabinets and on the metal table with four chairs.

"Can we head upstairs?" Sam wanted to show the Sheriff where Emmy was knocked out.

"No. Wait for me." Steve was writing in his notebook. "I won't be long."

He poked around the kitchen, looking into corners, inside cabinet doors and behind anything freestanding. Carefully, he pulled back the thin curtains on the windows and glanced at each sash. Locked with no signs of forced entry. Moving to the doorway separating the kitchen from the mudroom, Steve put away his flashlight. Sunlight poured through the open screen door and broken window panes. With only shelves holding a few canning jars, Steve's review of this area was brief.

"Bless you." Jenn yelled to him after she heard him sneeze. She knew the dust was activating Steve's allergies.

"Thanks, honey." Steve headed back into the kitchen when something fluttered, catching his eye. *Was that a leaf, or a butterfly?* Scanning the wood frame around the doorway, his eyes landed on a small piece of fabric. Plaid fabric. Blue, grey and tan plaid fabric, to be exact. He carefully pried it off the rough wood, placing it in a plastic bag. *Could be evidence.* Sealing the bag, he slipped it in the back of his notebook.

"Okay, let's all go upstairs." Steve led the group, noting carefully where the large boot prints were on each step, on the landing and in Emmy's room.

"Oh my," Emmy's voice was soft. Looking around her room, her eyes teared up. "Someone did make a mess." Instead of the books being back in the closet where she put them, several were strewn across the floor with pages torn or missing, just as Steve had told her. Even her beloved Heidi.

Picking up her favorite book carefully, she placed Heidi back in the closet. *What in the world...?* Her thoughts were interrupted by the conversation in the hallway.

"Same boot prints up here as downstairs," Sam was following the boot prints with his finger. "How did I not hear someone in boots going through the cottage and up the stairs?" He shook his head.

Steve, continuing to take notes, was mindful of the conversation. "It happens to the best of us; don't beat yourself up."

"Here's where someone escaped," Jenn pointed to the boot prints on the landing that led to the back window. "Look! There's even a print on the window sill." She peered out the window. "That's a long way down."

Steve squeezed in beside his wife and looked down. "Yep, a long way to jump. He may be hurt.

Hey, what's this?" He jiggled the window open and pulled at something.

"Is it a piece of fabric?" Jenn strained her neck to see.

"Yes. It's a piece of plaid fabric just like the one I found down in the mudroom. It may belong to the intruder, so it's definitely evidence now." He placed the torn bit of fabric with the other one in his notebook.

Whoever hurt Emmy and ripped her books apart left in quite a hurry, leaving part of their shirt behind. And whoever had done it was still running around loose.

# ~~ Chapter 5 ~~

"So it's settled, then. You'll stay here with us while you fix up the cottage." Jenn's big brown eyes twinkled. Happiness spread across her face as she smiled broadly and reached for Emmy's suitcase.

"Oh, I don't know – " Sam started.

"No. It's settled. You won't be far from work, and you need to be close to the cottage during renovations." Jenn caught Steve's eye and winked.

"Our extra bedroom and bathroom off of the family room will be perfect for you."

"It would certainly make things easier, but are you sure?" Emmy would like nothing better than to be closer to the cottage even though the commute was only 45 minutes from their home.

"Of course!" Jenn hugged Emmy. "We'll help you get more things from home later." Jenn walked toward the kitchen and paused. "It will be like old times but, instead of watching Granny bake brownies, we'll bake them ourselves!"

"What have we gotten ourselves into?" Steve and Sam shook hands and laughed.

Steve and Jenn had owned their house for a few years, buying it right after they were married. A small two story white farm house sitting on four acres, it boasted large windows, a wide front porch with rocking chairs, and a well-kept lawn. The addition of a family room, an extra bedroom and bathroom on the first floor gave them space for friends and relatives to visit who could enjoy a comfortable suite-like area of their own.

In the kitchen, Emmy helped Jenn fix a quick lunch of tomato soup and grilled cheese sandwiches.

"Nothing warms the soul like soup and grilled cheese." Emmy filled drink glasses with ice and poured freshly brewed tea for everyone.

"Come on guys, lunch is ready." Jenn called through the screen in the open window.

Steve and Sam were in deep conversation while their wives fixed lunch. Concentrating hard and keeping their voices low, they did not hear Jenn call them.

"Sam, I'm glad you decided to stay with us for a while." Steve kicked at some stones as they walked along the backyard path. "I'm sure we'll soon figure out what happened at the cottage; probably some bum just passing through looking for food or shelter."

"Yeah, the sooner the better. Renovating the cottage will be stressful enough. I don't want Emmy worrying about another attack." Sam furrowed his brow.

"I've got investigators working on leads back at the office," Steve assured Sam. "I'm keeping tabs on things in and around the cottage so we can – "

"Guys! Lunch is getting cold!" Jenn placed a bowl of lemon wedges on the table and motioned for the guys to hurry up.

The conversation slowed as they enjoyed lunch. Emmy was especially thankful for the warmth of the soup filling her up. She hadn't had much of an appetite since the hit on the head. Over lunch, future plans were discussed for catching up on work, shopping, hunting or fishing, renovations, and enjoying the spring and summer.

"Oh, excuse me." Emmy yawned. "Before heading back to the cottage, I need a nap." She carried her soup bowl to the sink. "Does anyone mind?"

"That's a great idea." Sam pushed away from the table, stood up, and grabbed his notebook. "We'll clean up, and I'll go over my notes. See you both in an hour."

Jenn walked Emmy and Sam to their room. Emmy paused as they walked past the built-in bookshelves in the family room.

"As soon as we get the cottage in decent livable shape, I'm buying more books!" Emmy smiled at Sam. "We'll need more bookshelves; you can build them for us."

Sam nodded. "Yes, Dear."

"I'll give you a few of these to start the new collection." Jenn laughed. "Make yourself at home and enjoy your nap."

Emmy took her shoes and socks off, tousled her hair, and crawled into bed. Finding the most comfortable spot, she sighed. Sam nestled his body in beside her, hugging her close to him. He smiled as he breathed in the faint scent of her perfume. His gentle kiss and soft touch calmed her fears as she drifted off to sleep.

~~~~~

"Boone, you're an idiot." Robert Cooper paced back and forth behind the shed near the cottage, wearing a path in the weeds. "You had one simple task."

"Come on man," Boone protested. "How's I supposed to know your cousin was going to be there snooping through the cottage like she owned it?"

Robbie Cooper was Emmy's cousin who, along with his brother Matt, spent a few summers at the cottage with Granny and Grandpa Charles. Their father, Jeremiah, and Emmy's mother, Sarah, were siblings and were the only children of Granny and Grandpa Charles. They loved their parents more than the cottage, especially as the cottage and both parents started showing their ages. They passed the fondness of visiting the cottage down to their children, but as the years went by and life became hectic, Emmy was the only grandchild to visit.

"She does own it. At least I think she does. She just doesn't know it." Robbie breathed in deeply and let out a long sigh. Looking at Boone's confused expression, he continued. "Right before Granny died, she rewrote her will. Thing is, not many people know because she hid it."

"Then how do *you* know Emmy owns the cottage?" Boone still looked confused.

Robbie had hoped to keep this little secret to himself. If all had gone according to plan, *his* plan, it would have remained his secret. Robbie knew he needed help to put his plan in motion. But he brought Boone into his plan, and that was a mistake. Boone and Robbie were casual friends but, occasionally after one too many beers, sometimes got into mischief.

"All the family came to visit Granny one last time as her health faded." Robbie talked fast to keep the story short. "We all knew her wishes and knew the will was in her lock box at the bank. After everyone left the cottage, I stepped back in to say a final goodbye. Granny was mumbling something – " Robbie poked Boone hard on the arm. "Boone! Pay attention; I'm only saying this once!"

"Ow! Sorry; I was just –" Boone rubbed his arm.

"Pay. Attention," Robbie continued sternly. "Granny was mumbling something so I leaned in close to hear her better. She kept repeating a phrase about 'timing and hiding the will in Emmy's cottage' over and over. I tried to tell her we knew the will was at the bank and Emmy had already visited, but she got more agitated. Then, plain as day, she said the cottage belonged to Emmy as listed in her new will and it was in the cottage."

"Where in the cottage?" Boone's eyes were open wide now.

"That's what you were supposed to find out!" Robbie rubbed his temples wondering how he got mixed up with this dimwit. "Remember, Boone? I paid you to snoop around and find the will. It turns out the lockbox was empty. But you had to get caught by – ” Suddenly Boone shoved Robbie down to the ground. “What the hell?”

“Shhhhh,” Boone covered his mouth. “Did you hear that?”

“Hear what? I was telling you about the will.” Robbie looked from behind the shed toward the cottage. It was dusk, but he could see there was movement inside and outside the cottage.

“Emmy and her friends are back.” Robbie’s shoulders slumped. He watched as Sam and Steve walked around outside and assumed Emmy and Jenn were inside. He motioned for Boone to step inside the shed so they wouldn’t be seen. They could keep watch through the window beside the shed door. Watching for Sam and Steve to walk around the side of the cottage back toward the front, they hunched down and waited.

“Girls, where are you?” Sam yelled coming in the cottage front door. “It will be dark soon.”

Emmy and Jenn had made their way upstairs after looking around downstairs. They were anxious to make plans for each room once Emmy and Sam bought the cottage. They were standing in the small window alcove at the top of the stairs envisioning a window seat and a reading nook when they both gasped. Something inside the shed darted by the shed window. The shed door burst open and just as quickly banged shut. A face appeared in the shed window, glanced around, and then disappeared.

As dusk settled in, Emmy and Jenn could just make out the outline of someone leaving the shed dragging something behind them. Something wrapped in a sheet. Something resembling a body.

~~~ Chapter 6 ~~~

The Middle Café was unusually busy tonight. It
was open for breakfast and lunch every day, but
only occasionally for dinner. As the cold winter
days drifted into warm spring and summer
evenings, residents and tourists of Middlebridge
took advantage of the season's longer days.
Farmers plowed and planted their fields. Kids
played soccer and baseball. Moms and dads
shopped in the main square and listened to bands

at various music venues. Having the café open some evenings helped Middlebridge keep the welcome mat out a little longer.

"Your imagination is in high gear tonight," Sam said smiling at Emmy. He grabbed the menu, opening it to the sandwiches section. He loved hearing Emmy tell a story; she left no doubt about any details and often made Sam feel as though he was part of the story.

"I know you think we're crazy, but Jenn and I swear we aren't making this up!" Emmy had talked non-stop on the short drive from the cottage to the café.

"I'm just saying you've had so much going on and a lot happening with the cottage, and maybe you didn't really see what you thought you saw." Sam gave Emmy the menu back and hugged her around her shoulders.

Jenn nodded. "It was getting dark and we're both tired. Maybe…"

"Steve, can you read back to us what you wrote in your notebook?" Emmy wasn't ready for defeat just yet.

"Can we order first? I'm hungry!" Steve closed his menu and motioned for the waitress.

The waitress, Missy, was a student at the local college, studying to be a teacher. She knew Jenn from assisting in her 6th grade classroom. She smiled as she hurried over to their booth.

"Hi! Good to see you all. What can I get for you?" Missy's enthusiastic smile was a welcome sight for the group. Emmy and Jenn ordered spinach salads and iced tea, while Sam and Steve ordered burgers, fries and beer.

Steve caught Emmy's anxious look and pulled out his notebook. Flipping to the page of notes from earlier that evening, he began reading.

"Alright. Sam and I were outside surveying the exterior of the cottage...looking at the siding, windows, the roof and such...trying to get an idea of what exterior renovations we could actually handle and which ones we'd need help with. We walked around the grounds a bit, but with the weed growth it was hard to really see much."

"You didn't see anything suspicious, like a path in the weeds toward the shed or someone around the shed?" Emmy's mind was still racing.

"No, I'm afraid not. It was getting dark." Steve continued, "Now, you and Jenn were in the cottage looking in the...in the kitchen, wasn't it? Is that where you saw something outside?" Steve flipped to another page in his notebook.

"We were upstairs when we saw someone in the shed," Jenn answered. "Emmy and I walked through the bedrooms, trying to envision furniture, window coverings and colors for each room."

"Well, we didn't see anyone right away. Remember?" Emmy began. "We were in different rooms and ended up in the small adjoining bathroom when we saw someone at the shed."

"The bathroom? I thought you said you were in the – " Sam stopped short as Missy arrived with plates of food and drinks. The conversation was temporarily replaced with mouthfuls of delicious food. The girls happily crunched the raw vegetables on their salads, and the guys bit deep into their warm juicy burgers. After several bites washed down with beer, Sam picked up where he left off.

"Weren't you in the alcove window? I think that's what I remember you said." He looked at Emmy and Jenn.

"The alcove window is what I have in my notes," Steve added. "Are you sure about that?"

"Uhm, yes. The alcove is right." Emmy took a long drink of her iced tea. "We were thinking about how a reading nook would be perfect there." She paused, then added, "We heard the shed door slam shut and looked –"

"No, the window was closed. I'm sure of that." Jenn interrupted. "We couldn't hear that far away being upstairs. We saw the door swing open then closed. I think." Her brow creased as she struggled to remember.

"I guess you're right." Emmy lowered her voice. "But we did see someone dragging a body out of the shed. What do we do about that?" *No sense in alarming the town. All sorts of nut jobs will start showing up at the cottage. My cottage, if we can get through this craziness and figure out a way to buy it.* Emmy glanced at Sam and smiled.

Steve and Sam looked at each other, then at the girls. Picking at the last of his french fries, Sam was ready to change the subject. It was becoming apparent both Emmy and Jenn were tired. They obviously saw something that startled them, but a body?

"Look," Steve said, hoping to settle things. "I know you saw something, and I believe you when you say you saw something. But, let's think rationally for a moment." He closed his notebook and drained the last of the beer out of his mug. "Even though there's been some trespassing, and Emmy was assaulted, I don't believe a body was dragged from the shed."

Jenn smiled at her husband then looked at Emmy. "He's being rational, you know. We're tired so we're being emotional." Pushing her empty salad plate away, she continued. "Didn't Granny store a few things in the shed besides canning and garden tools?"

Emmy thought for a moment and finished her iced tea. She did remember helping Granny cart items from the cottage to the shed. A broken ladder-back chair, some curtains and rods, a suitcase.

"Hey, I just remembered there were a few old rolled up carpets stored in the shed." Emmy sat up straight in her chair. "Could that be what we saw, Jenn? Someone dragging a roll of carpet out of the shed?"

"I bet that's it! Good job, honey." Sam paid the bill as they left Middle Café and walked down the street. "A roll of carpet slung over your shoulder could resemble a body."

"But it wasn't slung over a shoulder. It was being dragged out of the shed," Jenn added reluctantly. "Why would someone steal an old roll of carpet?"

"Why would someone steal Granny's pocket watch?" Emmy countered.

"Well, that's a little differ —" Sam slowed his walk as an older gentleman nearly ran over him on the sidewalk.

"Oh, excuse me, sir," the man panted. "I tried to catch you all as you left the café. I took a short cut but I guess I don't move as fast as I used to." After a moment, he caught his breath and continued. "I couldn't help overhearing your conversation about a cottage. A run down cottage. Would that be the Cooper cottage?"

"Yes, it is," Emmy responded, a shocked look on her face. "Emma and Charles Cooper were my grandparents. Did you know them?"

"You must be little Emmy!" The man's face lit up with delight. "Your grandparents talked about you all the time. I had the pleasure of eating some of your grandparent's homegrown vegetables. And homemade brownies." He smiled and patted his belly.

"I'm sorry. How did you know my grandparents?" Emmy smiled sweetly at the plump little man in front of her. "Have we met? You know my name but I don't know yours."

"Oh, no. Well yes, we've met. You were a small child, so I'm sure you don't remember. My how you've grown into a lovely lady. I helped them with some banking transactions many years ago." The man looked around. "Would you mind if we sat on this bench so I can rest?"

"Your name, sir?" Emmy asked as Sam and Steve helped him get comfortable on the bench.

"Oh yes! I'm Martin Smith, but you can call me Marty. I'm retired now, but dabble a little in real estate." His hands dug into his jacket pockets searching for his business card. Handing it to Sam, he continued. "I sure would love to see the Cooper cottage brought back to life. If I can help, I'd be so happy to."

"Thank you, Mr. Smith. Marty." Emmy was curious how he could help them with the cottage. "We have to find out who currently owns it and if they will sell it to us. It sure holds special memories for me."

Sam and Jenn had walked back to the café and were returning with a bottle of water for Marty. Handing it to him, he opened it and took a big gulp. The coolness felt good as it satisfied his thirst.

"I believe it's considered abandoned. That's where I think I can help you," Marty explained. "The past owners stopped paying taxes, couldn't sell it, and left." He took another drink of water. "If you will allow me to help you research it, we can find out if it's in foreclosure or if the county has condemned the property. Sometimes a condemned property can be sold for back taxes. The city or county gets money, you get the property for pennies on the dollar. Everyone's happy!"

"Oh, Sam! Wouldn't that be wonderful?" Emmy was already envisioning the cottage as hers.

"Yes, but let's think about it." Much to Emmy's surprise, Sam was cautious. "Marty, thank you for the information. We'll think things over and be in touch with you in a few days. May we reach you at the number on your card?"

"Yes. Yes, of course." Marty thanked them for the water. "Emmy, it's been my pleasure. I look forward to hearing from you real soon."

Marty waved goodbye and walked back toward the café as the others walked in the opposite direction to the car. People were still milling about enjoying the warm evening. He stopped to say hello to some of the kids at the ice cream stand and bought a cone for himself. As Marty was heading home, a figure slipped out of the shadows and followed him around the corner.

~~~ Chapter 7 ~~~

Sam forced himself to remain cautious about the process of taking ownership of the cottage. Emmy's excitement had finally won him over, but last night's encounter with this Marty guy was a bit of a surprise. Did he really know Granny and Grandpa Charles, or was something else going on? Marty seemed innocent enough, but Sam didn't need him throwing a wrench into the plans.

As a surprise for Emmy, Sam wanted to purchase the cottage for her. After they had been married and began talking about raising a family, the "buy a house or build a house" conversation frequently included the Cooper cottage. Sam knew what it meant to Emmy. Her love of family was one of the things he loved about her. He wasn't thrilled with the cottage's condition, but keeping it in the family and bringing it back to life was a challenge he and Emmy would gladly accept. They hadn't worked on a renovation project together for a while and Sam was ready to get this one going.

But first, he had to deal with Marty Smith.

Sam drove to town and parked in front of the Middle Café, hoping it would be a neutral place to meet Marty and discuss the cottage over a cup of coffee. Pulling out Marty's business card, Sam called the number.

"Hello Mr. Smith, I mean Marty, this is Sam Weston. We met last night; I'm Emmy's husband. Would you – "

"Who? Who is this?" Marty's voice was shaky.

"It's Sam Weston. Emmy's husband. Emmy Coo – "

"I'm sorry, I don't believe I know any Westons. Please leave me alone." The phone clicked and the line was silent.

*Great*, thought Sam. *I knew this guy was probably a quack. A salesman just trying to make a deal.* Wondering what he should do next, Sam walked into the Café and ordered a coffee to go. While waiting, he struck up a conversation with someone at the counter who was enjoying a slice of cherry pie. They chatted about sports, weather and local events. The waitress motioned for Sam and he excused himself to pay for and pick up his coffee, adding a slice of pie to go.

"I heard you talking with Gus. You mentioned Marty; Marty Smith?" The waitress handed Sam his change and placed the pie in a bag. "His office is just around the corner. He's retired, you know, but can't stay home. You'll probably find him in his office."

"In that case, I'll take another cup of coffee and a slice of pie to go." Sam smiled a thank you.

Sam walked down the street and around the corner looking for Smith Realty. He saw the business sign at the end of the row of buildings, just before a small park. He pushed the door open and stepped inside. It was a small place, comfortable and well-kept, but small. Two small chairs and a side table were all that could fit in the front waiting area. A small kitchenette, a desk and a chair sat toward the back. An open doorway on the back wall led to the filing area, which consisted of two vertical files, and beyond that a small bathroom. Sam set the coffee and pie on the counter.

"Well, hello there," Marty said coming out of the filing area. "Martin Smith. Call me Marty. How can I help you?"

"I'm sorry to bother you," Sam began, "I called earlier. How about some coffee?" Sam drank from his cup and offered the extra one to Marty. "There's also an extra slice of pie."

"Thank you. There's always time for coffee. And pie." Marty breathed in the coffee aroma from the steam and took a sip. "Were you interested in some property?"

"Yes. And I could use your help. It's the Cooper cottage. I'm Emmy's husband, Sam Weston. You followed us from the Café last night, remember?"

"Oh my, yes." Marty looked embarrassed and nervous. "You're the one who called. I did not recognize your name this morning. Of course I can help you! I've been looking at the paperwork for the cottage for a short time, hoping it would be rescued by someone. Not much there to research, but we'll take care of it. Oh, this is good news."

Marty excused himself and slipped into the filing area. Sam looked around, sipping on his coffee. Staring out the storefront window, he noticed a man across the street wearing a green jacket and sunglasses looking at the Smith Realty building. Not wanting to be recognized, the man ducked his head and quickly walked away.

"Let's see what I have in the file for the cottage." Marty interrupted Sam's thoughts as he came back to the desk and sat down. Marty shuffled papers around, stared at his computer and jotted down some notes. "Okay…uh-huh…yes, yes. Hmmm," Marty mumbled.

"Marty?" Sam wasn't sure if he should interrupt him or not.

Marty was deep in thought as he clicked the computer mouse, staring at the screen. "Well, I think I have good news," he began. "Oh. Do you have a question?"

"No, no go on, please. What's the good news?" Sam pulled one of the chairs from the waiting area closer to the desk.

Marty leaned back in his chair. "Charles Cooper passed away many years ago. His wife, Emma, lived quite a bit longer in the cottage enjoying family, friends, gardening and baking. She was – "

"Marty," Sam gently interrupted. "I'm married to their granddaughter, Emmy. I'm pretty sure I already know all about this."

"Yes, of course." Marty took another sip of coffee. "Well, after Emma passed, Charles' brother took possession of the cottage and property. Michael, I think was his name. Came from out of state."

"I didn't know Grandpa Charles had a brother." Sam raised his eyebrows and leaned closer.

"Yes, well, he kept to himself when he came to town. Didn't socialize much with the locals, but managed to keep the cottage and property in good shape. For a while at least. Then one summer, the grass wasn't mowed. When fall arrived, and the leaves fell, it was easy to see parts of the roof shingles and cedar shingles were missing. After another season of nothing being done, the cottage was in bad shape. Michael must of left town. Poor Emma would be so mad if she knew what her cottage looked like!"

Thinking out loud, Sam said, "Emmy never told me about this…this grand uncle, Michael. Why didn't Emmy's family, her mother, uncle, cousins step in and try to help? I thought they loved the place."

"Family can be funny sometimes; get their feelings hurt over the smallest things." Marty printed out some papers and handed them to Sam. "The good news for you and Emmy is just as I suspected. The documents here show Michael Cooper as the owner with no heirs listed. He's not been around here in years, repeated contacts from Middlebridge to a Michael Cooper over unpaid property taxes have gone unanswered. The cottage and property are in such bad shape so the town condemned it. As I mentioned last night, the town will be happy to get rid of the liability for the payment price of back taxes. $10,000. What do you think? Are you ready to buy the cottage?"

Sam's face broke into a wide smile. "Yes, Emmy will be thrilled, but is all this above board and legal?" Sam couldn't believe he and Emmy could own the cottage and five acres for just $10,000. Plus the thousands it would take to renovate it, of course.

"Perfectly legal." Marty smiled. "I'm happy to walk to the courthouse with you to complete the necessary paperwork and close the deal. Oh Emma would be so happy knowing her little Emmy was moving into the cottage and filling it with life again!"

Since it was her grandparents' cottage, Sam wanted Emmy to be a part of the entire process from the paperwork beginning, through the messy renovation middle to the move-in ending. Sam and Marty agreed to meet at the courthouse right after lunch. For Marty, that meant the rest of the morning would be devoted to gathering the necessary documents, and for Sam that meant finding a way to get Emmy downtown quickly for the surprise.

Reaching Emmy on her phone, Sam convinced her a lunch date was in order since she was window shopping nearby. He picked up some flowers from the florist shop next door to the Middle Café. Daisies, carnations, and tulips were some of her favorites. Emmy walked toward the café and a wide smile spread across her face when she saw him standing by his car, flowers in hand.

"What are these for?" Emmy took the flowers and breathed in their light fragrance.

"They're for my lovely bride." Sam hugged and kissed her. "And, to celebrate the fact we own the cottage. Well, almost."

"Whaaat? How?" Emmy couldn't believe what she was hearing.

"I called Marty Smith this morning. Apparently, the cottage was abandoned a few years ago. The cottage and property are ours if we pay the back taxes of $10,000. We can sign the paperwork this afternoon." A big silly grin spread across his face.

"I love you Samuel Weston!" Emmy threw her arms around his neck. "This is almost unbelievable." Out of the corner of her eye, she saw Jenn and Steve walking toward the café. She waved them over.

"Guess what? We're on our way to sign paperwork to buy the cottage!" Emmy hugged Jenn tightly. "Can you believe it?"

"That's wonderful, but we have some news." Jenn looked at Steve then back at Emmy. "I'm afraid – "

Steve stepped up. "I'm on my way to investigate a crime, a possible homicide. A body was found on an embankment by the South Bridge. It was wrapped in several sheets and blankets. Dirt was embedded along one area indicating it may have been dragged across the ground."

Looking at Jenn, Emmy blinked hard several times. "I knew we saw something that night!"

"Wow. I'm sorry to hear that, Steve. I don't mean to sound cold, but what does this mean for us about buying the cottage now?" Sam asked, reaching for Emmy's hand.

"Nothing that I'm aware of, buddy." Steve's voice was calm. "While the embankment is not far from the cottage, the body wasn't found on the property. No evidence at this time is connected between the two. You should be able to proceed as normal."

Emmy held tight to Sam's hand as she leaned against him and sighed. As much as she wanted to make the cottage a loveable home again, she now had second thoughts. First she was attacked, then Granny's pocket watch was stolen, now she and Jenn may have seen a dead body dragged from the shed and across the property.

Was someone trying to keep her from owning the cottage?

## ～ Chapter 8 ～

After a restless night, Sam convinced Emmy that it was okay for them to move forward with buying the cottage. As they sat in the county office building, he reminded her that Steve told them there appeared to be no evidence linking the cottage property to the body found by the bridge. It was just a coincidence.

"What's taking them so long?" Emmy paced the marble floor while they waited for the final documents from the clerk. "Do you think they found something in the property search records? I bet they did."

Sam pulled Emmy's hands into his and rubbed them. "Stay calm and take a deep breath. It's going to be fine, I'm sure." Sam held tight to her hands as she tried to pull away. "Sit here with me." She rested her head on his shoulder as his fingers gently ran through her hair.

Emmy looked around the waiting area. The county offices occupied the oldest commercial building in Middlebridge. Built in 1897, the front portico with Corinthian columns welcomed guests into the Classical Revival building. Tall triple hung windows, reaching high toward the ceiling, were topped in beautiful silk swag cornices. Emmy was the consulting historical designer when interior renovations were done two years ago. She worked tirelessly on the research of the timeline of the original construction to recommend fixtures and finishes that matched as close to the original as possible. Sam even worked on restoring and replicating some of the missing decorative details: door frames, wainscoting, pilasters. Even though she was a little bit anxious about the cottage paperwork, being here today brought back fond memories of the county office building project. She only hoped when she and Sam left the building, they would have their next project – the cottage.

"Ms. Cooper?" The deep voice startled Emmy as she jerked her head away from the comfort of Sam's shoulder. "Ms. Cooper?" The voice rang off of the marble tile.

"Yes; that's me!" Emmy said, walking quickly toward the tall, muscular man holding paperwork and impatiently looking around. "I mean, it's Mrs. Weston. Cooper is my grandparents' name. I'm Emmy Weston." She extended her hand and smiled. The man quickly shook her hand and motioned toward his office.

"Follow me. I have papers for you to sign." Emmy and Sam fell in step behind the county official, walking through two doors before arriving at his office. "Sit here." He motioned to two chairs with brown tweed upholstery worn thin in several spots, and placed haphazardly in front of his desk. "I'll be right back."

Sam's eyes scanned the sparsely furnished office, noticing the mismatched furniture and piles of paperwork in folders stacked around the office. A mug of day-old coffee sat on the corner of a dented file cabinet. "I guess Mr…whatever his name…is too busy with all this paperwork to worry about office furniture. He sure could use your touch around here, Emmy."

"Rodgers. His name is Stan Rodgers." Emmy pointed to a nameplate on the desk, half hidden behind some folders. "Two years ago, budget cuts didn't allow for many upgrades to office areas. Carpet and draperies were about it."

Mr. Rodgers stepped back into the office. Peering over the top rim of his glasses, he cleared his throat. "So you're buying the old Cooper place? It's been run down for a few years. You sure you want to do that?"

"Yes," Emmy began. "I've always—"

"You be careful, ma'am. Old homes can suck the life right out of you. Take all your money, too." Mr. Rodgers looked sternly at both Emmy and Sam. "Sometimes they're haunted."

"Thanks for your concern, Mr. Rodgers. Emmy has very fond memories of her time at the cottage. We look forward to fixing it up and living in it. Soon."

"Okay," Mr. Rodgers shrugged unenthusiastically. "Sign here where I've noted, make the check payable to the county, and the old place is yours."

Sam put his arm around her shoulders as Emmy's smile spread ear to ear. Twenty minutes later, they walked out of the office building as the new owners of the Cooper cottage. In the main lobby, a man wearing sunglasses stood behind a marble column watching them leave, careful not to be seen. As soon as Sam and Emmy were outside the building, he darted upstairs towards Mr. Rodgers' office.

~~~~~~

Jenn had been waiting by the cottage gate since school ended at 3:00. One of her 6th grade students wanted to talk about sports as they headed to the buses, so she had to hurry to get to the cottage. She and Steve were excited when they got the call that Sam and Emmy were the new owners of the cottage. Jenn practically knocked Emmy over as she greeted her with a big hug.

"Can you believe it's ours?" Emmy pulled away from Jenn's hug and stared at the neglected cottage. "Finally, Granny's cottage will be beautiful again. It will be a home again."

"Steve will be here later with some wine so we can celebrate," Jenn smiled.

"Sounds wonderful! While we wait, let's go inside." Emmy reached into the car through the open window and pulled out a small black case. "I brought my camera to take photographs to remind ourselves how bad things were. In the end, I'll take some more and make a scrapbook of before and after renovations."

"That's a great idea, Emmy!" Jenn glanced at Sam who was shaking his head. "I know how much Sam likes scrapbooking."

"Yeah, yeah. I don't mind it as long as Emmy does it. I'm happy to slap some photos in an album and be done with it." Sam winked at Emmy. "Come on. Let's go take some photographs."

Emmy began using her camera once they stepped inside. She wanted to capture as much as she could before the sun set. Once electricity was restored, she would re-photograph certain details without the natural light.

"You guys follow me, please. I don't want people in the initial photos," Emmy turned to face Jenn and Sam. "You will definitely be in the renovation photos."

Emmy crouched on the floor as she eyeballed the wood planks. They were dull, still covered in dust, some rotting with damage around edges closest to windows. Broken window panes had allowed wind and rain to blow in and settle. After replacing some boards, sanding, staining and applying a clear coat varnish, the floors would shine with life again.

Sam was writing down notes so Emmy could compare them with her photos. His fingers ran up and down window and door frames, feeling for cracks or sponginess from water damage. Anytime the floor squeaked, he wrote it down and asked Emmy to take a photo. Emmy and Sam both lingered around the built-in bookcases in the living room. Hand-made by Grandpa Charles, they were one of Emmy's favorite things about the cottage, and were still in great shape. Like the floors, sanding and staining would re-energize them. She couldn't wait to fill them with books and other family treasures.

"Hey, Steve is here," Sam saw his truck drive up and headed to the front door. "You girls keep taking photographs and I'll get Steve."

Emmy and Jenn headed toward the kitchen and began photographing the cabinets. Emmy and Sam planned to renovate the small kitchen into a larger kitchen/family room. Again keeping the original wood cabinets handcrafted by Grandpa Charles, they would add more cabinets to match details of the originals. A kitchen island topped with quartz stone would provide a visual separation between the kitchen and family room.

"I still love this space," Jenn's voice interrupted Emmy's thoughts. "Can't you just feel Granny's love?"

"Oh, yes; every time I step in here." Emmy walked around the square metal table, touching each chair, pausing to photograph them. As she stooped to look into the bottom cabinets, she found two wooden table legs from the dining table Grandpa Charles made. "Sam's project is to recreate the table top and other two legs."

"The sun is setting," Jenn touched Emmy's arm. "Should we go and come back in a few days?"

"Sure." Emmy slid her hand across the cabinet doors, feeling every detail. Her fingers lingered over one of the upper cabinet doors where the finish was worn. *"Don't close the door with your hand. Use the knob,"* she remembered Granny saying often. Turning to Jenn she said, "Remind me to tell Sam to keep this worn spot in the renovated cabinet door. It's a memory I want to keep and share with others."

The girls dusted themselves off and headed to the front porch just as their husbands were carefully making their way up the front steps.

"Steve has some news for us. Let's go over by the car." Sam reached his hand out to guide Emmy and Jenn down the porch steps. "It's about the body they found."

"I'll keep it brief so I can get back to the investigation." Steve pulled out his notebook and began reading. "The body has been identified as a young man named Boone. He was known as a drifter of sorts, coming to town looking for work when he needed money. He never got into much trouble, but wasn't very bright. He seemed to make bad choices." Steve sighed and continued. "The reason I wanted to tell you here, now, is—" He paused, looking at Emmy. "Do you remember the plaid fabric samples I gathered after you were assaulted? They match the shirt Boone was wearing when they found him by the bridge."

"What?!" Emmy's hand covered her mouth. "He's the one who assaulted me and took Granny's watch?"

"We didn't find the watch on him, but it's early in the investigation. I just wanted you to hear it from me first."

Sam pulled Emmy close to him, hugging her tight. As he did, an envelope fell out of his pocket. Picking the envelope up, Jenn handed it to Emmy.

"Oh, that was in one of the rocking chairs on the porch," Sam remembered. "It has your name on it, honey."

Emmy did not recognize the handwriting on the envelope as she opened it. Her hands shook as she read the note, printed in all capital letters: "STAY AWAY OR YOU'LL END UP LIKE BOONE."

# ~~ Chapter 9 ~~

For the next few days, Emmy and Sam worked on clearing out the cottage so renovations could begin in full force. Emmy had given Steve the envelope and threatening letter for the investigative file, and he was looking at every possible clue and suspect. Emmy and Sam planned to save as much woodwork, furniture, light fixtures and original door hardware as possible. Even though she tried to concentrate on the renovations, many thoughts swirled around in her head. *Where is Granny's watch? Who sent the letter? Who was this Boone person? Was it a mistake to buy the cottage?*

"Emmy!" Sam's terse voice, coming from the kitchen, snapped her back to the present. "I need your help!"

Emmy dropped the tools from her hands and ran from the living room to the kitchen. She caught herself as she slipped rounding the corner into the dining room. "What's wrong?" Are you—" Her eyes widened as she came into the kitchen.

The site of Sam with one foot on a ladder and the other perched on the counter top, slowly sliding, made her pause. The tiny bird, chirping, sitting on Sam's head made her laugh. Pulling her camera out of her pocket, she snapped several photos. "Say cheese!"

"A little help here, please, before I split my pants." Sam tensed his muscles to keep from sliding any faster. The chickadee hopped from Sam's head to the top of a cabinet close to the window. It chirped sweetly, thanking Sam for the moment of fun, and quickly flew out one of the broken window panes.

"I think you've made a friend," Emmy teased as she held the ladder and grabbed Sam's hand to steady him.

"We'll need to add screens to the list of things that are needed right away." Sam dusted his hands off on his pants. "It will keep birds and other critters out of here. Like mice or snakes." He playfully bopped Emmy's nose as she wrinkled it at the thought of mice and snakes.

"Let's take a break. You go to the hardware store and I'll go to the drug store. On my way back, I'll bring us some sandwiches." Emmy kissed Sam's nose and headed out.

Emmy parked her car in a spot not far from Ballard's Drug Store. It had opened in 1899, just two years after the county office building was built, and was still run by the Ballard family. Many places in Middlebridge were family owned and operated. The bookstore, the café, and a few antique/thrift stores to name a few.

"Good afternoon, Emmy. What brings you here today?" Tom Ballard was the fourth generation pharmacist in his family and knew many of the families in Middlebridge. The Ballards were well known for being compassionate and caring, treating most residents as part of their own family.

"Just some allergy medicine, Mr. Ballard." Emmy hugged him hello.

"Oh, yes. It is that time of year. I'll show you where we keep them." Mr. Ballard motioned for her to follow him.

Emmy and her cousins used to tag along with Granny to Ballard's. If they behaved, they were allowed to pick out a novelty toy or some candy. Matt and Robbie, because of their rowdiness, occasionally got a treat; Emmy always came away with something. Unlike the boys, she knew better than to wrestle in the aisle or bump into a display, spilling items onto the floor.

"I heard you bought your grandparent's cottage." Mr. Ballard turned around to face her after placing some items on a shelf. "I'm so glad it will be in good hands again. Your Granny and Grandpa Charles would certainly approve." His eyes twinkled as he smiled at Emmy.

"Thank you, Mr. Ballard. Sam and I are excited but nervous, too. Some funny things have been happening and I'm starting to wonder if we should have bought the cottage at all." Emmy placed the allergy medicine and some chocolate candy on the counter.

"Ahh, don't you worry. The cottage is where it should be. With you, my dear." Mr. Ballard rang up the items and gave Emmy her change back. "Why don't you go to the counter in the back and get you a milkshake. On the house."

"Oh, thank you. How sweet." Emmy tucked her hand inside Mr. Ballard's arm and followed him through the main aisle to the back counter, and looked over the small menu.

"Chocolate, vanilla, or strawberry is about all we have. Nothing fancy, but they are delicious and the best in the area," Mr. Ballard smiled proudly. "Excuse me while I help a customer who just came in. Lisa here will take good care of you."

Emmy chatted with Lisa and placed an order for one chocolate and one vanilla milkshake. To save some time, she also ordered two BLT sandwiches and french fries so she wouldn't have to make a stop at the Middle Café. Accepting the one free milkshake, and paying for the rest, she waved goodbye to Mr. Ballard as she left the drug store.

Emmy was heading to her car when a cool breeze beckoned her toward the park in the center of town. A walking path wound its way over gentle green slopes and between trees. Park benches were placed at various spots for relaxing or watching activities. She found an empty bench nestled in some forsythia bushes and sat down, placing the food in the shade. Several kids played in the grass running around, throwing Frisbees, or kicking balls. Ducks swam quietly across the small pond, rippling the water as they paddled by. A few moms pushed baby strollers. "One day that will be me with a stroller," Emmy smiled.

Knowing she couldn't stay long because of the milkshakes, she stood up to leave, but quickly sat down. Was that her name she heard? She remained seated and listened. The voice came from behind her on the other side of the forsythia bush.

"Yes, damn it. I said Emma Weston."

Emmy did not recognize the voice which sounded exasperated. *Should I stand and make myself known, or should I just sneak away?* Emmy's heart raced.

"She and her husband Sam bought the Cooper cottage. More like they stole it. It was supposed to belong to my client."

*Client? What client? And who was this person*

*talking about her on the other side of the bush?* Emmy strained to hear more.

"That Boone fella messed it up! Traipsing through the cottage probably leaving fingerprints everywhere, and who knows if someone saw him or recognized him. Hey, hang on a second."

Emmy had leaned a little too far forward, sliding off the bench and knocking over the bag of food. Hearing a lull in the conversation, she froze in place. *Did he see me or hear me fall? Can he hear me breathing?* She crouched trying to make herself smaller, feeling her heart beating in her chest.

"Here ya go, kid. Try to keep the ball on the grass." A soccer ball shot out from the corner of the bush sailing diagonally away from Emmy.

"We need to keep on our toes and stay one step ahead of Emmy and Sam. No one needs to get hurt, you hear me? And find out what "cub" means. That idiot Boone repeated it twice."

After a few minutes dragged on for what seemed like hours, Emmy realized there was no more conversation behind her. She sat still a little longer to let her heart rate slow down. Convinced she was alone, she stood, carefully peeked through the forsythia branches, and then around the side. Other than some kids walking by on the pathway, no one was there. Her hands shook as her fingers dialed Sam's number.

"Hey, honey. What's up? I hope you got some sandwiches because I'm—"

"I know where Granny's pocket watch is!" Emmy blurted out.

# ~~ *Chapter 10* ~~

"Good-bye, Ms. Haynes. See you tomorrow."
Jenn looked up from her desk as one of her
students stopped in her classroom doorway.
"Thank you for helping me today."

"You're welcome, Claire. Keep up the good
work. See you tomorrow!" Jenn waved goodbye
and packed up her briefcase. Checking her
voicemail, she gasped while listening to Emmy's
excited voice.

"I know you're still in class, but call me as soon as you get this; I think I know where Granny's pocket watch is!"

Jenn hurried to her car, anxious to call Emmy back. *I can't believe she knows where the watch is!* Jenn's face was beaming. She called and left Emmy a message that she would meet her at the cottage. Before reaching her car, Jenn made a quick stop at Grayson's Market for some produce.

Grayson's Market was primarily a fruits and vegetables farmer's market carrying fresh locally grown produce from the surrounding area. Like Ballard's' Drug Store, Grayson's was family owned and operated, and had been for over fifty years. Year round, especially during the off-season, they encourage people to sell their handmade or homemade products, whether they were greeting cards, jams, jellies and preserves, pickles, or cakes and pies.

Jenn gathered a few vegetables and placed them in her basket. She remembered the delicious cookies one of her teacher friends brought to school one day, and headed to the bakery section. Passing a counter holding stacks of jars filled with strawberry and peach preserves, Jenn took a strawberry one as a surprise for Steve. As she turned around, still reading the label, someone bumped hard into Jenn, knocking her back a step causing her to stumble. The jar dropped from her hands, sending shattered glass and gooey preserves to the floor in front of her. Gaining her balance, Jenn looked up at the male figure beside her.

"Hey! Look where you're going, why don't you?" The man's voice was gruff as he stared at Jenn. He was a little taller than she was, had broad shoulders and was a bit over weight. His hair, dark and unruly, spilled over his collar. His wrinkled shirt showed signs of wear and tear, and was not tucked into his jeans.

"Oh goodness. I didn't –", Jenn began, wiping her hands on her pants.

"Wait a minute," the man looked at Jenn, his eyes narrowing. "I recognize you."

"You do? I'm sorry, have we met?" Jenn took a step back away from the man and the mess on the floor.

"Yeah. You're a teacher and friends with that Weston girl, aren't you? Emily or something like that." He grabbed an apple from the display and took a bite, chewing loudly. "Jenny's your name, right? I hear Emily is fixing up the Cooper cottage. It wasn't supposed to be her place; you know she stole it. Are you helping her? Better be careful." His rambling and noisy chewing was annoying Jenn.

"Emmy bought it fair and square from the County. Why would you think she stole it?" Jenn took another step back as the man folded his arms over his chest. "It's hers and she can do what she wants with it."

Taking a final bite of the apple, the man stepped closer to Jenn. "Better be careful. *Jenny*." Throwing the apple core back in the display, he shoved his hands into his pockets. "Things can go wrong fixing up a house. You never know when there might be a water leak or a fire. Or someone might fall down the stairs." The smirk on his face made Jenn's skin crawl.

Before Jenn could say anything else, a familiar voice called out from behind her. "Is everything okay, Jenn?" Steve touched her shoulder and looked at the mess on the floor. "What happened here?"

"She's clumsy, I guess. I probably scared her." The man did not recognize Steve. "Women.

Always making a mess of something." Walking past Steve, the man grabbed another apple before heading toward the door. As he reached for the apple and turned to leave, Jenn grabbed Steve's arm.

"Did you see what was hanging out of his pocket?"

~~~~~

Emmy waited for Sam at the front gate of the cottage. *Where is he?* She was getting impatient with each step as she paced back and forth. *Did I hear that man in the park right or am I crazy?* She was ready to enter through the gate when Sam drove up. He rolled up the windows, grabbed a bag of potato chips and stepped out.

"I thought you'd never get here!" Emmy hugged Sam and grabbed his hand. "Follow me."

"Wait a minute, honey," Sam slowed down forcing her to look back at him. "Tell me what happened at the park. You said you know where Granny's pocket watch is?"

"Yes. Well, I think I do." Emmy began describing the events at the park. "Before going to the park, and while I was at the drug store, I decided to pick up some sandwiches – BLTs – and milkshakes. Oh no."

"What's wrong?" Sam's stomach growled at the thought of a BLT.

"In my rush to call you and leave the park, I left the food beside the bench I sat on." Emmy sighed. "Anyway, I stopped at the park on my way to the car, just for a minute. It's so nice out. I was watching the ducks on the pond and the kids kicking soccer balls."

"And that made you think about Granny's pocket watch?" Sam ate a few more potato chips from the bag.

"Not yet. But soon after I heard my name. A man behind me said my name!"

Sam frowned. "As in he called after you, trying to get your attention? Did you see him?"

"No, I didn't see him. He was on the phone with someone, said my name, and that you and I stole the cottage from his client."

"Client? What client?" Sam cocked his head to one side.

"I don't know. Then he said the name 'Boone'. That's the name of the guy they found dead by the bridge!"

"Wow. Unbelievable. We need to tell this to Steve." Sam was concerned these events involving the sale and renovation of the cottage were becoming a little too personal. "So how does this lead to Granny's pocket watch?"

Emmy turned to look at the cottage. "He said something that not very many people know about. He said Boone repeated a certain phrase a few times."

Sam narrowed his eyes. "Repeated a phrase? Like a secret phrase?"

"Not really a secret phrase, but one very few people know about. Cub. C-u-b. It's a phrase Granny used to say when we were kids. You know, when we were sad, angry, or scraped our knee. C-u-b. Chin up buttercup." Emmy smiled faintly at the memory.

"I see," Sam looked confused. "But, how does—"

"Come on, I'll show you!" Emmy grabbed Sam's hand and hurried around the corner toward the back yard. Navigating over cracked stepping stones, she stopped halfway to the shed and pointed. "Around the side is where Granny patiently taught me how to plant seeds for vegetables and flowers. She loved early spring flowers, especially daffodils. I'm sure there are some bulbs still left in the ground."

Sam followed Emmy to the far side of the shed. "How does this relate to the watch?"

Emmy's smile grew bigger. "I couldn't say daffodil when I was younger, so I called them buttercups. I bet her pocket watch is buried in that flower bed!"

"You can't be serious, Emmy! How would some stranger know about this, or even know about the meaning of cub?"

"I have no idea, but I'm willing to start looking. Maybe we'll find some more clues for Steve to investigate." Emmy got down on her hands and knees and began pulling weeds back to expose what was left of the flower bed. Knowing it was useless to argue with her, Sam joined her.

"I think we need something to dig with other than our hands," Sam said. "At least to break the hard top surface." He rummaged around some broken tools and found a small spade.

They carefully dug up old bulbs, some daffodils and some tulips.

"Careful!" Emmy said, finding pieces of glass. "We don't need deep cuts on our hands. These must be from Granny's canning jars."

"Hey, what's this?" Sam heard a clink as the spade dug into the ground. Laying it aside, they both began carefully sifting the dirt through their fingers. Sam felt something metal, dug deeper and gently tugged on it. Emmy sat back, eyes wide open. The dirt gave way and Sam pulled up a gold chain that was attached to a pocket watch. Granny's pocket watch.

"Oh Sam, that's it. Granny's watch!" Emmy's eyes filled with tears as Sam held the watch. "I can't believe we found it and that it was buried here." Wiping some of the dirt off her hands, she reached for the watch, anxious to hold it once again.

"I'll take that!" The voice came from behind them as someone grabbed the pocket watch from Sam's hand almost breaking the chain.

"Hey! What do you think you're doing?" Sam jumped to his feet.

"That's mine!" Grabbing for the watch, Emmy stumbled on the uneven ground she and Sam had just dug up. The man stepped aside letting Emmy fall. Sam reached to help her, but paused.

"Don't do anything stupid." The man patted the bulge on his side under his jacket. "You can't have both Granny's pocket watch and the cottage. That wouldn't be fair to Boone."

"Boone?" Emmy asked, rubbing her scrapped knee.

"Shut up! Both of you turn around, close your eyes, and count out loud to 50."

As Sam and Emmy began counting, the man quietly slipped away. After reaching the count of 31, Sam took a chance and peeked over his shoulder.

"He's gone, Emmy. How's your knee?" Sam held out his hand and helped her stand up.

"Fine. Just a little sore." Emmy rubbed her knee again. "I don't know who that was, but his voice is unmistakable. He's the one in the park who said my name!"

~~~ Chapter 11 ~~~

The more Jenn thought about the guy bumping into her at Grayson's Market, the madder she got. *Who does he think he is accusing Emmy of stealing the cottage? And what exactly did he mean by "stealing the cottage"?* Her mind raced with questions.

Jenn and Steve had left Grayson's after helping clean up the sticky mess from the dropped jar of strawberry preserves. Now, standing beside his

93

car, Steve was deep in conversation on the phone with someone from the sheriff's office, and Jenn was getting impatient. Her quick glances in Steve's direction told him to hurry. She wanted to tell him about Emmy's message, and to ask him many questions about the guy at Grayson's.

"Okay, if you're sure. I'll be in touch. A bewildered look crossed Steve's face as he finished the call. His eyes narrowed as he wrinkled hi brow. Turning to walk around the car, he nearly stumbled over Jenn.

"Steve!" Jenn said, leaning out of his way. "Did you hear me? Is everything okay?"

"Sorry, honey. I wasn't paying attention. The Sheriff has some interesting news."

"Well, so do I! Emmy called me at school and asked me to stop by the cottage as soon as I could. She may know where Granny's pocket watch is."

"What? Are you sure?" Steve jotted something in his notebook. "She found the watch?"

"Maybe. We need to get to the cottage now. She and Sam are already there."

Steve drove and made excellent time; it was no more than ten minutes later when they arrived at the cottage. Sam, walking around the side of the cottage, met them at the gate. He briefly shared the encounter with the man as they all made their way to the back yard.

"Oh, you poor thing!" Jenn hugged Emmy as soon as she saw her. "You found the pocket watch and right away someone took it? What on earth is going on?"

Steve listened and took notes as Emmy and Sam explained in detail what happened. Jenn's facial expressions amused them as he eyes opened wide in surprise, or her mouth gasped in frustration and disbelief.

"I really don't know," Emmy said when Steve asked her if she suspected anyone. "I just don't know who would care about Granny's pocket watch."

"Or, who would think you stole the cottage," Jenn added.

"How did you know about the man I saw at the park?" Emmy asked, looking directly at Jenn. "Well, I didn't see him. It's more like I heard him talking behind me."

"What man in the park?" Jenn looked confused. "I'm talking about the guy in Grayson's Market who accused you of stealing the cottage." Jenn glanced over at Steve. "Could it be these two men are one and the same?"

"The timing is a little close, but it's possible," Steve made more notes in his notebook about the two encounters.

"Steve," Jenn interrupted his writing. I forgot to remind you about what I saw at Grayson's. As the guy pulled his hands out of his pockets and turned to leave, he had something hanging out of one of the pockets. I'm pretty sure it was a piece of fabric. The same blue, grey, and tan fabric we found stuck to the window frame at the cottage."

~~~~~~

Steve headed back to the office to deal with the phone call he received earlier from the Sheriff. Armed with new details from Emmy's and Jenn's encounters, he needed to discuss the case, in particular Boone's death, with the other three investigators.

Emmy and Jenn headed back inside the cottage to talk about design details and what to start on first. Emmy showed Jenn the original items she and Sam planned to save: woodwork, a few pieces of furniture, light fixtures, and door hardware.

"I'm so glad to be a part of this renovation with you," Jenn smiled at Emmy. "Despite some of the crazy setbacks, it's going to be fun having you in the cottage. What a great tribute to Granny and Grandpa Charles."

"Yes, it will be fun." Emmy's sad eyes belied her enthusiasm. "I just hope nothing else goes wrong."

"What are your plans for the staircase, kitchen and bathrooms?" Jenn asked, trying to steer Emmy's thoughts toward design ideas. "Any carpeting or tile?"

Emmy walked over to the staircase and rubbed her hand across the newel post and partway up the bannister rail.

"No carpeting on the staircase. We plan to repair the risers that need it, strip the old finish, and re-finish the wood to bring out the beauty of the dark oak."

"Sounds great," Jenn agreed, shaking her head up and down. "Floors, too?"

Oh, yes," said Emmy, a twinkle returning to her eyes. "Granny took pride in her oak floors. We'll repair and re-finish the floors, and use area rugs for color."

The wood of the bookcases showed promise as they walked passed them in the living room, wiping dust off.

"These may not need much repair," said Jenn. "Grandpa Charles' good craftsmanship has held up pretty well. Let's head to the kitchen."

Emmy recently jotted down some ideas for the kitchen, but had not had a chance to share them with Sam. She looked around and began talking her way through the kitchen.

"We'll keep as many of the cabinets as we can, repairing the frames, and re-finishing all the doors. We'll have to replace all the appliances, but will make sure the new ones give an appropriate nod to the era. We both want a farm sink, and perhaps a large red cook stove." Emmy looked back at Jenn and smiled.

"I love those ideas!" Jenn smiled broadly. "What about the counters? Will you go retro and use Formica, similar to what Granny had?"

"I don't think so. Sam and I talked about a fun tile or soapstone. But—"

"But, what?" Jenn was intrigued by Emmy's playful pause. "Tell me!"

Emmy walked to the opposite side of the kitchen and opened one of the drawers. Pulling out a small brown bag, she handed it to Jenn.

"What is this?" Jenn asked, carefully looking in the bag. "It's broken."

Emmy helped pour some of the contents out of the bag and into Jenn's hands. Picking up a few of the pieces, Emmy laid them on the counter in a pattern.

Jenn tilted her head to the left. "Are they pieces of pottery?"

"Yes. They're pieces of pottery Granny collected over the years. I found some pieces in the shed, outside the shed, and here in some of the kitchen cabinets. After collecting them, I realized we could use them to make a tile mosaic in the kitchen. If there are enough, we can use them on the counters; if not, then maybe as the backsplash."

"What fun! I absolutely love that idea!" Jenn hugged Emmy tight. "Better yet, Granny loves that idea."

"I'm so glad I thought of saving these broken pieces when I found them. I think Sam will love the idea, too." Emmy carefully placed the pieces back in the bag, and back in the drawer. "Speaking of Sam, let's see what he's up to outside."

Jenn followed Emmy out the back door as they maneuvered carefully over the patio stones. While the girls talked design ideas inside, Sam stayed outside to clear away brush and think about landscape ideas.

The vegetable garden area, long overgrown, was still discernable by the indention in the ground. Sam decided, if Emmy agreed, to keep the garden in the same area close to the shed. Even though the shed was in sad shape, it could be salvaged.

Grandpa Charles had planted several apple trees when Emmy was young. She and her cousins, Matt and Robbie, liked to climb up their own tree and throw apples at each other. They made sure to use apples that had already fallen from the trees because those could be used by Granny for applesauce or fried apples. Sam decided a few apple trees could be salvaged, as well.

Sam waved and motioned for Emmy and Jenn to join him. They followed the path he made through the weeds to the middle of the back yard.

"I've got some ideas for the vegetable garden, and we can keep some of the apple trees." Sam pointed to the side of the cottage. "Think about what plants you want to put there, Emmy. And we can relocate some flower bulbs to the sides or front of the cottage."

"We'll be busy for years getting this place fixed up," Emmy sighed at the thought of all that lay ahead. "But, it will be worth it. I hope."

"It will definitely be worth it," Jenn chimed in. "And don't forget that Steve and I are here to help."

"Of course we're here to help." Steve was back from the office and had followed the path around the cottage looking for them. "But, I'm afraid I have some bad news."

"What is it this time?" Sam asked. "Did you find Granny's pocket watch broken and thrown away?"

"No. I wish it were that simple." Steve looked at Emmy. "I need to ask you to come to the sheriff's office with me to answer some questions."

"What..? What questions?" Emmy stepped toward Sam and grabbed his hand.

"Steve," Sam started. "What's going on?" He squeezed Emmy's hand.

"Just some routine questions. I'll be with you, Emmy, and guide you through. You'll be fine."

"Routine questions about what?" Emmy's voice waivered.

Steve explained the situation in a manner that Emmy would understand. "Someone has filed a complaint against you concerning the cottage and the missing pocket watch. The many clues and evidence I've gathered so far seem to support that."

"You can't be serious!" Emmy couldn't believe what she was hearing. Wasn't *she* the one who was knocked out and had the watch stolen from her?

Sam put his arm around Emmy and looked at Steve. "Buddy, I know you're doing your job. But, are you sure this is a legitimate complaint? You know Emmy wouldn't hurt anyone or steal anything. Right?"

"Of course I do," Steve said, almost insulted. "This is the part of my job I don't like. Sam and Jenn can come and stay with you, Emmy. Trust me, please?"

Sam let go of Emmy's hand and wrapped his arms around her, holding her tight. She nestled her face against his shirt, feeling the warmth of his chest as his hand caressed her hair. Tears balanced on the edges of her closed eyes, eventually breaking free to roll gently down her cheeks. Soon, her shoulders trembled as the tears turned into sobs drenching Sam's shirt.

# ~~ Chapter 12 ~~

Late afternoon, between the lunch and dinner crowds, was not a very busy time at the Middle Café. It gave the cooks and wait staff time to catch their breath, and it gave people who came in during that time a place to read or talk quietly.

A few people sat at the counter, drinking coffee, enjoying a slice of pie, or reading the newspaper. A man sat in the corner booth far from the front door. If he was trying to be inconspicuous, his darting eyes and fidgety fingers gave him away. A man came in the front door, walked toward the corner booth, and slid in the seat across from him.

"Hey, Boss Man. About time you showed up. What's up with hat and glasses?" He laughed loudly, reaching over to tap the hat brim. Not amused, Boss Man smacked his hand away.

"Keep your voice down," Boss Man hissed, glaring at his friend. "You want everyone to know our business?" He took off the hat and laid it next to him on the booth seat. The dark glasses stayed on his face. "So tell me what happened."

"Well—" Before his friend could start, a new waitress smiled as she came over to take their order.

"What will it be fellas?" The waitress clicked her pen and flipped open her order pad.

"Nothing. We're just here to talk," Boss Man snapped.

"Hey. Maybe you're not hungry, but I am. I ain't talking until I eat."

Glaring at his friend, Boss Man relented. "Fine. Bring us a couple of burgers and beers." Still glaring, he looked at his friend. "Now talk. What happened?"

"Well, I followed Emmy just like you told me to. She sure didn't make it easy. In and around town, to the drugstore, to the park. The park! I thought she saw me for sure. Then finally to the cottage."

"You're sure she didn't see you?" Boss Man asked, questioning his friend's ability to hide.

"Absolutely. I was...oh good, our food is here." He took a bite of his burger and motioned for the waitress to come back. "Can you bring us some fries? Thanks, hon."

Boss Man took a long swallow of his beer and let the smoothness slide down his throat. He laid his head back against the booth. "Go on. Then what?"

Chewing another bite of burger, his friend continued. "After reaching the cottage, I crouched and hid in some tall weeds, and watched Emmy and her husband walk around to the back. I carefully followed and stopped at the back corner of the cottage and patio. Oh, thanks." He nodded at the waitress. "These fries smell great."

He dipped some fries in ketchup and stuffed them in his mouth. After wiping his greasy fingers on his jeans, he continued.

"I watched them digging in the dirt for a while, moving from spot to spot. I crept closer so I could hear them. *'Blah, blah this; blah blah that.'* They were so excited when they dug up the pocket watch! It almost felt cruel to take it from them." He washed the fries down with a gulp of beer. "But I took it anyway."

Boss Man smiled and stuck out his hand. "Let me see it."

The man pulled the watch out of his pocket and handed it to his friend. "Just one question, Boss Man." He admired the pocket watch once more before releasing the chain. "How did you know where the watch was?"

Boss Man pulled a few bills out of his wallet to pay for their food. Looking his friend straight in the eyes, and with a smirk on his face he said, "Just a lucky guess."

~~~~~

As upset as Emmy was at having to go down to the sheriff's office, she was still keenly aware of how drab the interrogation room was. The pale grey walls were scuffed from years of chair backs rubbing against them. The light brown carpet, worn in several places, was stained with what appeared to be coffee. A variety of mismatched chairs sat around a utilitarian conference table with a chipped green laminate top.

Trying to reassure Emmy, Steve motioned toward a chair and pulled it away from the table. "This is the most comfortable one. How about some coffee?"

No thanks, Steve. I'd like to get this over with as soon as possible." Emmy sat and stared down at the table.

"Of course. This is mainly a fact-finding meeting. Sam, you and Jenn can stay. Just sit at the other end of the table and don't say anything." Nodding in agreement, they both sat down. Jenn sent a nervous reassuring smile to Emmy.

Steve sat at one end of the table and placed a file folder and his notebook in front of him. "Along with the notes I've gathered, I also had the clerk pull some files on the history of the Cooper cottage. Looks like your grandparents owned it free and clear until they died."

"Yes, that's right," Emmy nodded at Steve.

"And it was passed down to their children. Is that correct?" Steve flipped back and forth through paperwork.

"Yes. Well, I think so. Having their own homes, Mom and her brother didn't want the cottage. To everyone's surprise, no will could be found even though Granny and Grandpa had everything else in order. At least we thought they did." Emmy took a long pause. "The family fought over property taxes and who should pay them. The cottage just sat there. Empty." Emmy closed her eyes and rested her head in her hands.

After giving Emmy a minute, Steve continued. "The complaint that was filed said you stole the cottage. Why would someone say that?"

"I don't know. How can it be stolen if we bought it from the county? Is that in your records?"

"Yes, it states $10,000 was paid to cover back taxes. Emmy, was anyone else aware of the low purchase price?" Steve slightly raised his eyebrows.

"Are you accusing us of a sneaky deal?" Sam couldn't keep quiet anymore. "We made a deal fair and square, and paid what the county wanted."

"I'm not accusing anyone of anything, Sam. Just doing my job and gathering facts." Steve turned to another page in his notebook. "Tell me about the pocket watch, Emmy. You said it was stolen when someone surprised you upstairs in the cottage?"

"Yes," Emmy thought back to that day. "I was upstairs in my room, looking at the daisy wallpaper, and thinking of how much I missed my grandparents. I moved some of the dusty books around and before I knew it, WAM, someone hit me on the head. I remember seeing a glimpse of something shiny as I fell. I think it was the chain on Granny's pocket watch. He must have seen it among the books as he snooped in the closet."

"Are you sure it was Granny's pocket watch?" Steve looked hard at Emmy. "Could it have been something else? His own watch, maybe?"

"Why? Is this guy claiming I stole his watch, too?' Emmy half laughed. "Granny had a small hiding place in the closet where she would hide surprises for me when I visited as a kid. Candy, toys, stuff like that." Emmy paused a moment. "I found the watch one day and she told me to leave it there as our little secret. It should have been on the shelf in the closet, but it wasn't. Yes, I'm sure it was Granny's."

Steve thought for a moment before moving on. "Why would he steal the pocket watch? Just for the joy of stealing something or for another reason?"

"Wait a minute!" Emmy suddenly sat up straight. Reaching into her purse, she pulled out a piece of folded, worn paper. "I didn't think of this until all these questions were coming at me." She showed it to Steve. "When I moved books around in my room, this fell out of one of them. It's written in Granny's handwriting." Gently unfolding the note, Emmy began reading out loud.

*Shadows of time for the journey home*
*Enjoy what you see even when alone.*
*New life will be given to all you have loved*
*Time will tell the truth as noted above.*

# ~~ Chapter 13 ~~

A good night's sleep is what Emmy and Sam needed after being subjected to so many questions from Steve. Emmy hoped she never had to see the inside of a sheriff's office again. None of them knew what Granny's note meant. *Why was it in a book and what on earth does it mean?* Even though Emmy slept well, she went to bed thinking about the note and woke up thinking about the note. She grabbed he robe and headed downstairs.

"Hey beautiful," Sam kissed Emmy good morning, and brushed a wayward strand of hair off her forehead. As they hugged, he looked into her eyes. "You're squinting. What's going on inside of that pretty little head of yours?"

Emmy smiled. "You always did know when I was deep in thought."

"Good morning!" Jenn sang as she came into the kitchen. Having Emmy and Sam stay with her and Steve meant they frequently had breakfast together. "Chef Steve will be down any minute. Same menu as usual? Pancakes, eggs, and bacon?"

"Yes!" Sam answered, barely giving Jenn time to finish.

"Not for me. I'm going to grab a quick bite of toast and strawberry jam, and a cup of hot tea," Emmy said. "I want to get back to the cottage; I have so many ideas running through my mind."

"Oh, honey, why rush? Let's have a good breakfast then go to the cottage. Can't you wait a little while?" Sam's sad-looking eyes made Emmy laugh.

"You can have whatever Chef Steve fixes and then join me at the cottage. Now that we've started clearing away debris and weeds, I'm anxious to get it renovated and move in." Emmy poured hot water from the tea kettle over her tea bag, and reached for the jam.

"Chef Steve at your service, Steve announced as he stepped into the kitchen, tying an apron around his waist. "Nothing is off limits, as long as it's pancakes, eggs and bacon." His hearty laughter filled the kitchen as he gathered the ingredients for breakfast.

"Nothing for me, thanks." Emmy took the last bite of her toast. "I'm headed to the cottage." She turned to Sam as she drained the tea from her cup. "Enjoy your breakfast. Meet me at the cottage in about an hour?"

"Sure. Just be careful." Sam hugged Emmy. "And don't start ripping out walls until I get there. Promise?"

"Promise." Emmy smiled and waved as she headed upstairs to change out of her robe and slippers.

After Emmy left, Steve turned his attention to fixing breakfast for Jenn and Sam. Steve welcomed any opportunity to cook for family and friends. Grilling steaks or chicken was his favorite, but cooking breakfast came in as a close second. Cooking provided a creative outlet that Steve didn't get from his investigative duties with the sheriff's office.

"Sam, there are still some uneven spots in the cottage floors. Will Emmy be okay alone at the cottage?" Jenn asked as she finished her meal and cleared the table. "I can go over there now to help her." She gathered the dishes while Sam grabbed the eggs, jam, and butter, and put them back in the refrigerator.

"She'll be fine," Sam answered. "She knows the rough spots well enough to be extra careful when roaming around. It will do her some good to be there by herself envisioning what it will look like after renovations." He swallowed the last sip of his coffee. "Once again Steve, another great meal. We look forward to doing this at the cottage soon."

Steve flashed a proud smile, wiped the flour off his hands, and shook Sam's hand. "Anytime buddy. Do you want us to meet you at the cottage? We can finish cleaning up later."

"Thanks, but not today. How about tomorrow? I think Emmy wants to plan out a few ideas she's been tossing around. I want to bounce a few thoughts of my own off her, too. You both can help us once we narrow down our ideas." Sam headed upstairs to change into work clothes.

~~~~~

Emmy arrived at the cottage full of hope. She'd answered all of Steve's questions at the sheriff's office, and was sure whoever filed the complaint was just trying to scare her into giving up the cottage. *It's probably some big developer wanting to build a lot of cheap condos. Well, not this time and not this place.* Emmy was determined to honor Granny's and Grandpa Charles' memory with bringing life back into the cottage.

She wanted to wander around for a little bit with no agenda until Sam arrived. Then they would make more definitive plans for each project. For now, it was just Emmy and her thoughts. Wandering from room to room on the main level she started her furnishings list: a rocking chair by the fireplace, cushions for the window seat, area rugs for most rooms. No full carpeting was going to cover the beautiful wood floors once they were refinished.

Emmy headed to the staircase so she could go upstairs to the bedrooms. Several cracked bannisters caught her eye so she made some notes for repairs or replacements. It was late morning, breezy, and sunny. Several windows tried to let in sunlight but not much got through the dirty, dusty panes. As she examined the newel post, she heard a creaking sound coming from the back of the cottage.

"Hello," Emmy called from the bottom of the stairs in the front of the cottage. "Sam? Has it been an hour already?"

No one responded. She waited another minute, eyeing a few cracks in the plaster wall. *I love the look and feel of plaster walls, but repairs are so difficult.*

"Sam, I'm headed upstairs to my room."

At the top of the landing, she heard another creak that sounded like it was overhead. Was someone on the roof? Just then a tree branch sailed by the small window. *I guess we'll need to get used to the wind and the things it blows by the cottage.*

Emmy walked into her room, the daisy

wallpaper smiling a cheery "hello" to her. She made a note to definitely replace the aging paper with something as close to the original as possible. Granny would be pleased. She walked around the room and decided a small, fully upholstered rocking chair would be a perfect addition. Another sound snapped her attention away from the wallpaper and rocking chair.

"Sam?"

Again, no one answered.

Emmy heard footsteps downstairs that sounded like someone was roaming and getting closer. She listened more intently as she tried to quiet her breathing. If it were someone, it couldn't be Sam. He would have answered her greeting. A chill crept over her and she wanted to run away as fast as she could.

The footsteps grew quieter as though they were leaving, and Emmy let out a soft sigh. Maybe someone stopped to peek into the cottage thinking it was still abandoned. *The next important thing on our to-do list is to clear the front yard and make the cottage looked lived in.*

A door creaked open. Or had it creaked closed? Emmy drew in a sharp breath as she started to tremble. She decided she needed to get out of the cottage if a prowler was snooping around. She tiptoed out of her bedroom toward the upstairs landing. She eased down the stairs hugging the wall. She was almost at the bottom when the stair tread creaked louder than the door had a moment ago. She froze in place, but not for long. The sudden sound of feet running toward her from the back of the cottage propelled her back up the stairs.

"Stay away from me!" She screamed as someone grabbed at her and she kicked them away. She stumbled a little on the stairs trying to regain her balance. That split second allowed her assailant to grab her and pull her back down the stairs.

"Take it easy now. Don't fight me so hard and you won't get hurt." The grip tightened around Emmy's arm.

The familiar voice stung Emmy's ears. Her muscles clenched, and her head snapped around as she forced herself to look at the man behind the voice.

"What are you doing here, Robbie?" She glared at him. She tried to pull away but his grip tightened even more.

"I'm looking for something, but that's none of your business." His eyes were dark; not the friendly ones she knew growing up.

"Maybe I can help you find it," Emmy said, trying to think of a way to break free.

"Ha! I don't need your help, or anyone else's for that matter. Every time someone tries to 'help' me, I get screwed." He loosened his grip on Emmy's arm a little and helped her stand up.

Emmy remembered Sam was on his way and decided the best thing to do was keep Robbie talking. "What are you looking for?" Maybe he knew about Granny's pocket watch and was after that to sell it for some quick cash. If only she knew where it was.

"Why should I tell you? You think you know everything, but you're not as smart as you look, dear cousin." Robbie guided Emmy down the last few steps and into the living room. She glanced around for something she could grab as a weapon, and remembered she and Sam had taken everything out of this room on their last visit. *Sam, please hurry.*

"Robbie, why are you doing this? Granny and

Grandpa Charles would be so disappointed. Don't you remember the good times we had here?"

"Of course I do, and this cottage should be mine." Anger returned to Robbie's eyes. "Granny promised me—" He stopped short and stared through Emmy. "You wouldn't understand because you were her favorite."

"Robbie, don't say that. She didn't have favorites; she loved us all. Maybe each in our own way, but—what did you just say?"

"I said no one would even miss you," Robbie was holding a small iron pipe he had hidden in his jacket. "It would look like you had an unfortunate accident while trying to fix up a dilapidated house."

"Robbie! You don't want a murder on your hands." With any luck Sam would be at the cottage in a few minutes, but Emmy had to think fast. She didn't like the look on her cousin's face. "Robbie, listen to me."

"Shut up! It's too late. If that idiot Boone had found what I asked him to look for, he would still be alive and none of this mess would be happening." Robbie held firm to Emmy's arm and the iron pipe.

"Boone?" The realization of what Robbie was about to say hit Emmy hard. "You killed Boone?"

"He messed up everything!" Robbie shouted and raised the pipe at Emmy.

In a flash, without thinking, Emmy threw a rock at Robbie that she had picked up and hidden in her pocket. It found its mark on one of his eyes making him swear in pain and drop his grip on her arm. He was still ranting, blinking both eyes when Emmy raced out the front door running right over Sam.

"Whoa, what's wrong?" Sam said as he kept Emmy from tumbling off the front porch.

"Robbie. Inside." She mumbled through heavy breathing. "He killed Boone and he's trying to kill me!"

~~ *Chapter 14* ~~

"Wait a minute. Slow down, I can barely understand you!" Jenn asked Emmy twice to repeat her story. "Are you okay?"

Emmy had run off the front porch, through the front gate, and out to the car. She begged Sam not to go after Robbie.

"We need Steve at the cottage now. Please tell him to hurry!" Emmy's voice was still shaky. "I'm afraid Robbie may kill Sam!"

"Robbie?! What is he—"

"Hurry Jenn!" Emmy cut the conversation short, and hid behind the car to catch her breath.

Inside the cottage, Sam was standing just to the left of the front door wondering which way Robbie ran, and where he might be hiding. *What is going on with Robbie, and why is he trying to hurt Emmy, his own cousin?* Sam had a bad feeling about confronting Robbie. Not knowing if Robbie was armed with more than an iron pipe, Sam picked up an old 2X4 in case he needed to use something as protection. He stood there quietly listening. Sam hoped Robbie would be the one to make the first sound, and he prayed his thundering heartbeat wouldn't give himself away.

After several minutes of not hearing or seeing anything, Sam tiptoed into the living room. His attention was immediately drawn to the footprints on the dusty floorboards. The footprints, scattered in a haphazard pattern, would not lead Sam to any clues because several people over the last few days had walked through the cottage.

Sam slowly made his way to the fireplace on the opposite wall of the living room. The sun was covered by clouds making the cottage dark. He felt his way along the mantle and made it to the back corner of the room. From that vantage point, Sam could see the front entry on the right. He could partially see the dining room on the left, and through the doorway, he could see part of the kitchen. For a brief moment, Sam let his thoughts drift to the list of projects he wanted to do to the cottage. Some of the more difficult ones he would need help with, such as re-wiring and re-plumbing. He knew his favorite project was going to be a surprise for Emmy: re-tiling the kitchen backsplash and the fireplace surround.

Sam stepped a little closer to the fireplace to look at the tile when he heard a creaking noise from the kitchen area. Was that Robbie still inside, or the cottage settling? As he turned, his hand hit against the loose tile sending one crashing to the floor. *Damn*, Sam thought silently to himself as he froze in place.

Sam stood up straighter as he heard another creak, this one coming from the direction of the front entry. Or was it the staircase? He wasn't thinking clearly, and his grip on the 2X4 tightened.

The distinct sound of heavy footprints on the stairs rang in Sam's ears. He moved quickly toward the entry. Peering around the corner, Sam saw a male figure a quarter of the way up the stairs fumbling with something in his pocket.

As the man turned, Sam recognized it was Robbie. Sam watched as Robbie bent to pick up something that dropped from his pocket.

"No!" Sam yelled, as Robbie picked up a match book. Anger blinded Sam, and he lunged at Robbie, catching him off guard. "What are you trying to do?!"

The force knocked both men off their feet and down the few steps to the bottom landing. Kicking his way free to stand up, Robbie glared at Sam. "Damn you! Stop wasting my time!" Robbie swung a fist at Sam, but missed.

Robbie's heavy boots fell across the creaky floor as he started to head back upstairs. Without warning, he suddenly turned and shoved one of his boots into Sam's side, causing Sam to double over in pain.

"I'm going to take what's mine!" Robbie yelled right into Sam's face. The splitting pain, and the aroma of stale beer on Robbie's breath, made Sam wince. Robbie took advantage of the few extra seconds and ran upstairs.

Sam's ribs were on fire, but he was pretty sure they weren't broken, only bruised. He slowly stood and caught his breath. A loud crash and cursing from upstirs told Sam that Robbie had tripped over something. Sam knew he needed to get upstairs quickly if Robbie was planning to set fire to the cottage. *Emmy, I hope you got a hold of Steve.*

Sam rushed upstairs with the 2X4 while gingerly holding his side. He hoped the 2X4 would come out the winner over Robbie's iron pipe. He turned the corner into Emmy's room, but stopped short. "Robbie!"

Robbie was bent over a small pile of papers in the middle of the room. He reached into his pocket for some matches, and as he pulled his hand out, several items fell to the floor. Robbie quickly reached for the matches and Sam grabbed the item that rolled his way: Granny's pocket watch.

"Not so fast." Robbie staggered a little, but was staring directly at Sam. "That's my ticket outta here." He pulled out a gun and aimed it squarely at Sam's head.

Sam closed his eyes and swung the 2X4 at the same time the gun angrily erupted to life. The bullet hit the 2X4, knocking Sam to the floor and causing him to drop the 2X4. Sam laid on the floor for a moment, stunned, waiting for the next shot.

There was nothing but silence.

Sam's ears were ringing.

"Robbie?"

Silence.

Sam carefully raised himself up on his elbow, and saw Robbie lying on the floor spread eagle on his back. Sam inched closer, and breathed a sigh a relief when he saw Robbie's chest gently rise and fall with steady, shallow breathing.

~~~~~~

Emmy frowned. "It just doesn't make any sense." She sat with Sam as he nursed his sore ribs. "I don't understand why Robbie couldn't leave well enough alone. There's no reason he needed to do this."

Emmy and Sam went home with Jenn after Sam was checked out by paramedics. As he suspected, his ribs were bruised and not broken.

Steve had arrived at the cottage shortly before he heard the gunshot. He had spoken to Emmy outside telling her to get away from the cottage and stay with Jenn, who was down the road at the next driveway waiting for her. He had called for backup and would go inside when someone arrived. As soon as heard the shot, he pulled his weapon and ran inside yelling for Sam.

Searching the bottom floor carefully, he yelled for Sam again. That time he heard movement from the second floor. Maneuvering up the dusty stair steps, and into Emmy's old room, he found Sam on the floor looking at Robbie's body.

"Too bad I couldn't hear you." Sam smiled at Steve. "I hope I'm never that close to a gunshot again." His smile faded as he moved to a more comfortable position.

"What's going to happen to Robbie?" Emmy was mad at her cousin, but still sympathetic. "Will we ever get settled in the cottage, and will I finally get Granny's pocket watch back?"

Steve had interviewed Robbie extensively after the paramedics checked him out. Robbie had a bloody gash on his head, requiring several stitches. The bullet had ricocheted off the 2X4 causing a large piece to snap off. The force of the broken piece of wood caught Robbie by surprise, and he had been knocked unconscious.

"Well when interviewed, he confessed to many things, which helps us solve several crimes." Steve sat down across from Emmy and Sam. "It appears jealousy and hard times are the root of his problems. Throw in a little bit of bad luck, and anyone might snap."

"Jealousy? For what?" Emmy was confused. She and her cousin may have fallen out of touch over the years, but she wasn't aware of any underlying ill will.

"According to his statement made at the sheriff's office, the hard times started when he was laid off from his job last year. The downsizing within the local government positions hit a broad swath across all levels of employment, so his manager position was not spared." Steve took a sip of water and continued. "He started to drink more and after a long time of not finding another job, he lost his home."

"Wow. I had no idea." Emmy sighed.

"He then got the bright idea that he could live in the cottage, since it was abandoned. Maybe fix it up." Steve continued, referring to his notes. "But then you and Sam started snooping around."

"Snooping? You make it sound like we were

out to do damage!" Emmy defended herself.

"Just reading my notes of what Robbie said," Steve smiled. "He was the one snooping around."

"Really? What was he looking for?" Sam moved gingerly, but his ribs reminded him that he moved too fast.

Steve looked directly at Emmy. "Your grandmother's will."

"What?!" Emmy was stunned.

"Robbie was under the impression your grandmother had hidden a new will in the cottage. He wanted to be the one to find it."

"I, I don't know what to say –" Emmy shook her head.

"Was he the jerk that hit Emmy over the head?!" Sam's eyes narrowed as he started to think back.

"Not according to him," Steve answered. "He convinced that guy Boone to rummage through the cottage in hopes of finding the will. Boone hit Emmy. All he found was Granny's pocket watch."

Emmy hesitated, looking at Jenn, but knew she needed to ask. "Did Robbie kill Boone?"

"Yes, but he swears it was an accident." Steve said.

"Ha! Ohhh—" Sam blurted out before remembering his sore ribs. "I don't believe him."

"Time will tell us as the investigation winds up."

"All those mishaps and coincidences were part of Robbie's plan? A plan to frame me for something *he* did so he could get away with—"

"Murder!" Jenn interrupted.

"Yes, murder, but also stealing property he thought should belong to him." Emmy said.

"The cottage and property belong to you, Emmy." Steve said, turning around grabbing a bag of items to show them. He laid it on the table.

"Of course it belongs to them," Jenn said. "They bought it from the county."

Steve handed Emmy the bag of items. In it was Granny's broken pocket watch, a few notes, and an envelope.

"The watch fell out of Robbie's pocket as he fumbled with the matches," Steve explained. "The fall caused the watch to split open, and Sam grabbed it trying to save it."

"Yes, but Robbie didn't want me to have it. I guess he thought he could sell it and get some cash." Sam added.

"That would have been the best thing for him to do. Now we know the secret." Steve said.

Emmy, Jenn, and Sam looked at Steve, tilting their heads in unison. "We do?" Sam asked.

Steve explained that one of the investigator technicians noticed markings on the interior of the pocket watch. He researched further and found out the markings were similar to old combinations on bank lock boxes, before they used keys.

"As part of the investigation, the technician worked with the bank managers to find and search their old lock boxes. Bingo." Steve said with a smile. "The markings were the combination numbers to your Granny's lock box."

"But, how can you know for sure?" Emmy stared at Steve in disbelief.

"By piecing together the evidence I collected, it all fell into place. The clincher was the note you gave me that fell out of one of your books. Remember? It mentioned 'shadows of time' and 'time will tell the truth'. I believe Granny used her pocket watch as a code for you."

"And Robbie knew this?" Sam asked.

"No, I don't think so," Steve answered. "He just thought the watch was worth some money."

"But, that doesn't explain how the cottage belongs to me, outside of us buying it," Emmy reminded Steve.

Steve handed her the last item from the bag, an envelope. "This explains it."

Emmy looked at Sam with tears in her eyes as she opened the envelope.

"Granny's will!" she gasped. "Jenn, please read it for me."

Jenn began:

*I, Emma Rosalie Cooper, residing in Middlebridge, Virginia, being of sound mind and sound body, do hereby declare that this is my last will and testament. I give all of my estate to my only granddaughter, Emma "Emmy" Weston. It is a wonderful privilege to pass along my worldly goods to you, as you possess what I cherish the most: love, integrity, and a generous heart. With this privilege comes great responsibility. That is why I have chosen you.*
*Love, Granny*

Sam broke the silence. "Wow. How about that."

Emmy wiped away tears and smiled.

"I wonder if you can get your $10,000 back?" Jenn asked.

"Not if it was used to pay back taxes to the county." Steve added. "Besides, that just gives you and Sam extra protection to prove the cottage really does belong to you guys."

Emmy slid over to Sam and curled up next to him. She gently slipped her arm around his side, and felt the warmth of his body against hers. He rested his cheek on her head which was nestled under his chin.

"I cannot wait until we move full steam ahead on the renovations," Sam said. "Our future kids will love growing up in it as much as you did, Emmy. Especially our daughter."

"A daughter, huh? You sound so sure." Emmy chided.

"I am. And her name will be Rosalie." Sam leaned down and kissed Emmy. "We'll call her Rose, for short."

"Welcome home, Emmy and Sam", Jenn smiled. "Welcome home."

## ~ DEDICATION ~

This book is dedicated to my family. Whether that is my "born into" family, "married into" family, "raised from birth, or by choice" family or "friends for life" family. I wouldn't be who or where I am today without you. The love of family is a blessing. I am blessed.

# ~ ACKNOWLEDGMENTS ~

This book would not have been realized without the generous support of the following people:

Lois Allen Hawthorne, my mother, who believes in me and encourages me in all things. Close friends and family, whose continuous love, support, and laughter carried me through the years. Wayne Drumheller, writer, editor and photographer extraordinaire, whose talent skillfully helped me move this project forward. Benjamin Sears, my editor, whose kindness and generosity of time and talent made me a better writer. Last but certainly not least, Wayne Ponton, my wonderful husband, who is my biggest supporter and the love of my life. Not for just a day. Not for just a year. *Always.*

# ~ ABOUT THE AUTHOR ~

Lori Hawthorne Ponton is the author of *Framed for Murder*, the first in "A Cozy Cottage Mystery" series. This is her first published work of fiction. Among her experiences, she is a certified interior designer, a furniture buyer, an antiques buff, a clarinet player, and an avid scrapbooker of life's journey.

Lori grew up in southern West Virginia, graduated from West Virginia University and moved to central Virginia. There she built her career as an interior designer and furniture buyer, met her wonderful husband and raised (so far...) three dogs, two cats and one son. She enjoys traveling, reading a good book on a rainy or snowy day, listening to jazz/swing/big band music, and a nice glass of wine. She also enjoys watching and/or attending WVU Mountaineer football games, all things chocolate, and any movie starring Sean Connery. Early on, she sharpened her design skills with Barbie's Dream House and her reading/writing skills with Nancy Drew mystery books.

Lori lives in the foothills of Virginia's Blue Ridge Mountains (close to friends and family) with her husband and beloved pets. While those pets mainly include dogs and cats, occasionally they also include the deer and rabbits that repeatedly (year after year) enjoy her vegetable garden as much as she does!

The author can be reached at:

lori.hawthorne.ponton.author@gmail.com
*or*
www.facebook.com/LoriHawthornePonton-Author